Xmas.

To Kenneth-H

From

Frank

"Now boys," shouted Frank, "over the top and at them!"

Army Boys in France

OR

From Training Camp to Trenches

BY

HOMER RANDALL

Author of "Army Boys in the French Trenches" and
"Army Boys on the Firing Line"

ILLUSTRATED BY
ROBERT GASTON HERBERT

NEW YORK
GEORGE SULLY & COMPANY
PUBLISHERS

ARMY BOYS IN FRANCE

CONTENTS

iii

CONTENTS

ARMY BOYS IN FRANCE

CHAPTER I

THE BUGLE CALLS

"Looks like war, fellows!" exclaimed Frank Sheldon, as, on a cold March morning he came briskly into the business house where he was employed, and slipped off his overcoat.

"Oh, I don't know," responded Bart Raymond, Frank's special chum. "It's looked like war ever since the *Lusitania* was sunk, but we haven't got our fighting clothes on yet. The American eagle keeps on cooing like a dove."

"He's waking up now though," asserted Frank confidently, "and pretty soon he'll begin to scream. And when he does there'll be trouble for the Kaiser."

"He isn't worrying much about us," put in Tom Bradford. "He figures that his U-boats will do the trick long before we get ready to fight. Sometimes I think he's pretty nearly right too. They're sinking ships right and left. They got three of them yesterday, and one was a liner of more than ten thousand tons."

I

"That's bad," agreed Frank. "But the worst thing about it is that one of the three was an American ship. As long as they sank only French and English vessels, it might be said that it was none of our business, although it has always seemed to me a cruel and cowardly way of fighting. But when they get after Uncle Sam's boats it's time for us to get busy."

"Johnny get your gun! get your gun!" chanted "Reddy," the irrepressible office boy.

"What's the use of talking," said Bart disgustedly. "They'll cook up some excuse about not knowing that it was an American ship, and we'll swallow the excuse and pretend to believe it. One lie more or less is nothing to a nation that calls a treaty a scrap of paper."

"It wasn't that way in the old days," remarked old Peterson, the head bookkeeper, who had been at the "Bloody Angle" when Pickett led the charge at Gettysburg. "Men were men then and ready to fight at the drop of a hat. Americans didn't need a swift kick then to get them into action."

He shook his gray head mournfully at the thought of the evil days on which his country had fallen.

"Don't you worry, Mr. Peterson," replied Frank confidently. "America is just as sound at heart as ever she was. Just let the bugle

call and a million men will answer. We'll raise
an army in less than no time."

"Well, perhaps so," admitted Peterson half
grudgingly. "But even if we did they'd be raw
troops and stand no chance against trained soldiers. They'd only be food for cannon. It
takes at least a year to make a soldier. And
before we could get on the firing line the Germans might have France and England licked to
a frazzle."

"Not much chance of that," put in Tom. "It's
more likely to be the other way. What's Hindenburg doing now but retreating?"

"But it's a long, long way before he'll get
back to the Rhine," replied Peterson. "And in
the meantime it looks as if Russia was getting
ready to quit. I tell you, boys, if we get into
it, the work of winning the war will be on our
shoulders. And it won't be a cinch any way
you look at it."

"Not a cinch perhaps," agreed Frank thoughtfully, "but I wouldn't have any doubt about
how it would come out in the long run. I'd back
America to whip the world."

"So would I," came back Peterson promptly,
"if it were just a question of man against man.
But this is a war of machinery. The day's
gone by when a man could grab a musket and
run out to meet the other fellow who, as a

rule, wasn't any better prepared than he was. Now it's a matter of cannon, and machine guns, and liquid fire, and poison gases, and all the rest of it. The Germans have those things and know how to use them. We haven't got them and wouldn't know how to use them if we had. Why, a single German army corps has more machine guns than we have in the whole United States!"

"Of course we're not prepared," broke in Hal Chase. "But we've got plenty of company in that. Who in the world was prepared except Germany? She caught all Europe asleep. If three years ago anyone had said this war was coming we'd have thought him crazy."

"Yes," agreed Tom. "That's true enough and you can't blame the rest of the world too much. But there's no excuse for us being caught this way. We've watched this thing developing for the last two years and coming closer and closer to us all the time. It was a dead sure thing that sooner or later we would get in it. And yet we've been like a man who sees the house next door burning and doesn't take any steps to protect his own."

"Well," said Frank, "what's past is past and there's no use crying over spilled milk. There's no use either in asking who has been to blame. That can be settled after the war. What we

Americans have got to do is to buck up, stand shoulder to shoulder, and fight as Americans always have fought when they've got into a scrap."

"Sure thing," agreed Bart. "But just now it would be like a man fighting with his bare fists against another fellow that's got a gun. He might be brave enough, but the other fellow's bullet would get to him before his fist could land."

"It isn't the first time we've been in this fix," said Tom. "But somehow or other we've always managed to come through on top. See how it was in 1812. We didn't have any navy and England had the greatest fleet in the world. But we built the ships and made the guns, and knocked spots out of the other fellows."

"Yes," said Hal, "and Perry won the battle of Lake Erie with ships made from trees that a hundred days before had had birds' nests in them. And what we did once we can do again."

"You've said it!" broke in Reddy, who, although too young to be a soldier, was chock full of patriotism.

"Oh, well," said old Peterson. "We're not in the war yet and perhaps we never shall be. But there will be war sure enough if the boss comes in and finds you fellows chinning when you ought to be working. So get busy."

"How about Peterson himself?" said Bart to Frank in a lowered tone as they scattered for their tasks. "I notice the old chap himself isn't slow when it comes to a talk fest."

The firm of Moore and Thomas, by which the young men were employed, did a thriving hardware business in the prosperous town of Camport, an inland city of about twenty-five thousand people. The work was wholesale and extended all over the country. They carried on also quite an export trade, and just now because of the war feeling that was in the air they were busier than usual. So that for the rest of the morning the boys kept close to their work, and conversation was limited strictly to business.

But the thought that was in all their minds could not be long suppressed, and the discussion broke out afresh when twelve o'clock struck and they knocked off work preparatory to going to lunch.

"I don't think we'll wear these duds much longer," remarked Bart as he put on his coat. "I'll bet most of this bunch will be in khaki before three months are over."

"I know one that will anyway," replied Frank. "Just let the President call for troops and I'll come running."

"Oh, you fellows make me tired!" broke in

a rough voice behind them. "All the running you'll do will be to run away when you get sight of a German uniform."

They wheeled around and saw that the speaker was Nick Rabig, the foreman of the shipping department.

He was a big burly fellow with a mottled face, thick neck and small eyes that seldom had in them anything but a surly expression. He was the bully of the place, and was universally disliked.

"Who asked you to butt in?" demanded Bart, nettled at the interruption.

"This is a free country, ain't it?" replied Rabig, truculently.

"Sure it is," said Bart. "That's the reason your father came here from Germany, wasn't it?"

The shot went home, for Rabig, though born in this country, was of German descent and for the last two years had been vehement in his denunciation of the Allies and fervent in his praise of the Teutons

"Germany's all right," he retorted, "and don't you forget it!"

"If Germany's all right, it's surprising how many Germans try to get away from it," remarked Frank dryly. "You don't notice many Americans going over to Germany."

"That's just because Germany is crowded," defended Rabig. "But just the same it's a better country than America ever dared to be. And when she gets through this war she'll be twice as big as she was before and there'll be plenty of room for all her people."

"Going to gobble up all Europe, is she?" asked Frank, sarcastically.

"Then I suppose she'll come over and take in America, too, so as to make a good job of it," said Bart, with a grin of derision.

"Why not?" responded Rabig, promptly. "Somebody has got to rule the world, and why not Germany?"

Quite a group had gathered about them by this time, and there was a roar of laughter at this frank expression of the German spirit and the German purpose.

Rabig grew red with fury. His little eyes glowered as he glared about him.

"We'll hang the Kaiser on a sour apple tree!" chanted Reddy.

Rabig aimed a blow at him which Reddy adroitly ducked, and Frank stepped between them.

"Leave the boy alone, Rabig," he demanded, and Rabig's fury turned on Frank.

"What have you got to say about it?" he snarled. "Do you want to fight?"

CHAPTER II

A REMORSELESS ENEMY

THERE was a murmur of excited expectation and the crowd gathered closer.

For a full minute Frank's eyes looked full into Rabig's. And in the silent duel Rabig's eyes were the first to waver. Then Frank spoke.

"No," he said, quietly. "Brawling isn't in my line. I won't fight—not here or now."

There was a sigh of disappointment from the onlookers who had been keyed up in delighted anticipation, and Rabig, though his eyes had fallen before the glint in Frank's, resumed his swaggering air.

"Afraid to fight, eh?" he sneered.

Before a reply could be made, Mr. Thomas, the junior member of the firm, came out from his private office and the gathering dispersed.

"Why didn't you trim him, Frank?" asked Bart curiously, as they walked down the street together. "I wanted to see you wipe up the ground with him. You could have done it too. You've got as much muscle as he has and ten times the grit. I fairly ached to see you sail into him."

"Well," said Frank, thoughtfully, "there were two reasons. In the first place, I didn't care to soil my hands with the fellow and put myself on his level. Then again, you know how sensitive my mother is, and she'd have hated to see me get mixed up in a shop brawl. But Rabig has his coming to him, and he'll get it sooner or later."

"Sooner, I hope," returned Bart. "If you don't, I'll do it myself. That *"Deutschland Uber Alles"* stuff of his is getting on my nerves. Just now it's the ambition of my life to lick a Hun."

"You may have the chance sooner than you think," laughed Frank. "Germany's just about got to the end of her rope with us. Let her sink just one more ship and she'll find out what she's up against."

"It can't come too soon for me," responded Bart, and as just then they reached the junction of the streets where their ways parted Bart went on and Frank turned into the quiet street on which his home was located.

It was a modest little structure, set some distance back from the street, surrounded by flowers and shrubbery which in summer were a riot of color and perfume.

Before his hand touched the door knob, his mother, who had been watching for his coming, swung the door wide open and stood ready to give him a loving greeting.

Frank's eyes brightened as they dwelt upon her. She was a pretty little woman with a piquancy of expression, a brightness of eye and an alertness of carriage that at first glance betrayed her French origin. Her pretty color and a certain appealing helplessness in her manner toward her son had always made her seem to Frank more like a charming sister than a mother.

And now as he put his arm protectingly about her and stooped to kiss her he was alarmed at the traces of recent tears which she had not been able entirely to obliterate.

"Mother!" he cried, holding her away from him and searching her face anxiously. "You've been crying! You just tell me who's made you, and I'll—" he doubled up his fist in a threatening gesture; but with a little laugh his mother inserted her own small fingers within his and led him into the dining-room.

"Look!" she cried, pointing to a great steaming tureen of soup that stood in the center of the table. "You said last night you were hungry for soup, and so I made it especially for you, dear, to surprise you. You must tell me how you like it before you ask any more questions. See, how steaming hot it is."

"Say, and I stopped to argue when this was waiting for me!" cried Frank, literally flinging himself upon the tempting dish. "Run around to your side, Mother, and hold your plate. Say, if this tastes as good as it smells—"

Like two children they tasted the soup, then with expressions of contentment laughed into each other's eyes. Then Frank launched into an account of the morning's events, for he was accustomed to discuss everything with his mother, who was his comrade in all things small or great.

"My fingers itched to be at that bully," he said, "but I held myself in, and I guess you know one of the reasons."

"Yes, dear," responded his mother, lovingly. "You're always thinking of me. I'm glad you didn't get into a fight. I have always hated them. A time may come," she added, a shadow crossing her face, "when you will be forced to fight, not for yourself, but for the honor of your dear country."

"For two countries, maybe," said Frank with a smile. "For every stroke that America deals to the Kaiser will help France as well."

"Ah, *la belle* France," said his mother with a sigh. "How my heart bleeds for my beloved country! I had a letter to-day from Cousin Lucie. And, oh, she had such terrible news!"

"Nothing has happened to her, I hope," said Frank, quickly.

"No, not to her," replied his mother. "One of those poor refugees from Belgium has got through the German lines and is staying at her house. This woman was at Dinant when the town was captured by the Germans in the early part of the war, and the stories she tells of what happened there are too dreadful for words. And yet she saw those things herself, and Lucie tells me she is sure the woman is honest and tells the absolute truth."

"I am ready to believe almost anything of German brutality," said Frank, bitterly. "And I suppose for every awful thing that's told there are a hundred more that haven't come to light. Tell me what Cousin Lucie said."

"This Mrs. Pentlivre," replied his mother, "told Lucie that the Germans attacked the town early on an August morning. They outnumbered the defenders, who were forced to retreat and take up new positions. Then those Huns entered the town.

"It was about half past six in the morning. The cathedral was full of worshippers, as it was Sunday and services were being held. The Germans burst into the church, drove out

the people and separated the men from the
women with the butts of their rifles. Then
the troops deliberately shot into the mass of
unarmed men, killing twenty or more of them.
They made prisoners of the rest, and then
went through street after street, setting all
the houses on fire until the beautiful town was
completely destroyed.

"All day long they kept the wretched people
prisoners, threatening and reviling them—you
couldn't imagine the names they called them,
so Cousin Lucie said—and after that they
took all the people whom they had not already
put to death to a garden wall at the end of
the town. Then they took those poor men and
even the little boys and stood them up against
the wall. Oh, Frank, what do you suppose
those murderers did then? Shot them down in
cold blood, while their wives and mothers fell
shrieking on their knees, begging passionately
for mercy for their loved ones."

"The brutes!" cried Frank, pushing back his
chair and beginning to pace the room while his
mother watched him with tears in her eyes.
"There's German Kultur for you! And what
they did there, they've done in fifty other
places in Belgium and Northern France. I tell
you, Mother, the world won't be a fit place to
live in until such things are punished as they
ought to be."

"I'm afraid not," sighed his mother. "But such a task as it is going to be!"

"America will do it!" cried Frank, confidently. "It's up to her to tame the beasts. France and England are holding them in check, but they won't be able to drive them back until Uncle Sam's army boys get over there."

"But think of what it means if we get into the war," said his mother sadly. "It's bad enough to read and hear about such terrible things, but what will it be when our own men are killed and wounded and blinded by the thousands. Ah, I cannot bear to think of it!" and she looked at Frank with apprehension in her eyes.

"Americans have always known how to die," said Frank, proudly. "They've shown that at Bunker Hill, at Monterey and Gettysburg and other battlefields. And the man who doesn't know how to die, doesn't know how to live and isn't fit to live."

"Spoken like my own brave boy," cried his mother. "And yet my heart stands still when I think of you in those awful trenches. You are all I have, Frank!" and tears welled again to her eyes.

"I know, little Mother," said Frank, coming around to her chair and patting her cheek fondly. "But you wouldn't want your son to be a slacker, would you? How could I look you in the face if I held back, while the sons of other mothers went forward to fight for their country."

"You're right, dear, of course," said his mother. "And hard as it would be, I'd let you go if your country needed you. But, oh, the days and nights of waiting while you were gone! I would not have one happy moment, one care-free hour."

"Yours would be the harder part, Mother," said the son gently. "I'd have at least the excitement and fury of the fight, while you would be eating out your heart here—alone. But cheer up," he continued in a lighter tone, "it hasn't come to that yet, and perhaps it never will. A hundred things may happen. Russia may come up to the scratch again. Hindenburg has already begun to retreat, Germany may cave in at any time. Austria may make a separate peace. The Germans may call off their U-boat campaign rather than bring the United States into the war. We'll hope for the best while we're getting ready for the worst. At any rate, we won't grizzle about it till we have to—will we, Mother?" this last in a coaxing tone that brought a swift response from his mother, whose French vivacity and sparkle returned in a measure.

"No, we won't, dear," she answered, smilingly brushing away the tears. "We're going to be just as happy and bright as ever and await with courage whatever the future may bring to us. But, dear boy, look at that clock! You'll be late if you don't hurry. Hurry, now, I must not be the one to blame."

She kissed him good-bye with a smile on her lips and waved to him merrily from the doorway. But there was a world of foreboding in her mother eyes as she watched him swinging briskly down the street.

CHAPTER III

THE GATHERING STORM

Events moved on swiftly for the next few days. History was being made at a more rapid rate than ever before. War was in the air and everybody felt it.

"Something's got to break mighty soon, Bart," remarked Frank, as he met his friend one morning.

"Can't come too soon for me," said Bart. "Ever since we broke off diplomatic relations I've known there could be but one end to it. That's never been done yet without a country finally going to war."

"And it won't this time either," agreed Frank. "The fact is, I'd be almost sorry if it did. I'm getting so sore at the way the Germans are trying to ride rough shod over the world that I'm anxious to get a whack at them."

"I, too," declared Bart. "The cool way in which they offered part of the United States to Mexico has got me so riled that I can't think of anything else but getting even. And you notice how, in spite of all warning, they keep

18

on sinking American ships! They figure that we're just bluffing. Their newspapers keep telling them that we're only a nation of shop-keepers who think of nothing but the almighty dollar and that we're making so much money out of the war in selling munitions to the Allies we'll take good care not to get into it ourselves."

"They're just about due to wake up out of their dream," said Frank, grimly. "They make a big mistake when they think our patience is cowardice, or greed for money. As a matter of fact, there isn't a nation in the world so unselfish as America. Look at the way we went into the Spanish war—just pure humanity, to save Cuba from the horrors she was undergoing at the hands of that butcher, Weyler. And see how quickly we gave Cuba her independence as soon as the war was over and she was ready for it. There isn't another nation in the world that would have let such a rich prize slip through her fingers when once she had laid her hands on it."

"Oh, well, the Germans are fed up on lies, anyway," responded Bart. "That's the only way the government can keep up the spirits of the people. The newspapers say just what the Kaiser tells them to say. Some day the papers will tell them that the Americans have horns

and hoofs, and they'll swallow it without wink-
ing."

"They'll see for themselves what we are,"
said Frank, "when our boys go over the top
and meet them face to face."

"I just got a letter from Billy Waldon," went
on Bart. "He's been down on the Mexican
border chasing Villa and his gang. Says he's
in fine shape and feeling like a two-year-old.
His regiment's been ordered back, and he'll be
with us soon. Says he's honing to get a crack
at the Germans."

"Billy's a fine fellow," said Frank heartily,
"and the experience he's been getting in Mexico ought to help him a lot when he gets in the
French trenches, if he ever does."

"He'll get there all right," asserted Bart. "I
hear that the first thing the Government will do
will be to put the national guard regiments in
the regular army. You know the old Thirty-
seventh that Billy belongs to is mostly made up
of Camport boys. I've half a mind to join myself as soon as they get back."

"That might not be a half bad idea," said
Frank. "Although my own thought was that
as soon as the President called for troops I'd
join the regular army at once. But it's as broad
as it is long, for, as you say, the first thing the
Government is likely to do is to make regulars

regulars of the national guard. And it won't
be a bad thing either, for they've had lots of
drilling and will be a heap better at the start
than raw recruits who don't know the first
thing about a gun."

"This experience the boys have had on the
border hasn't done them any harm either," replied Bart. "Of course most of them haven't
had any fighting to do, but they've had to be
prepared to fight and the outdoor life has made
them tough and strong. Billy says you'll hardly
know the boys for the same fellows when they
get back."

"Oh they're a lot of heroes—I don't think,"
sneered Nick Rabig, who was working near by
and had heard part of the conversation.

"What do you mean by that?" asked Frank
indignantly.

"Just what I say," retorted Rabig. "They
went down to Mexico to catch Villa, didn't
they? Well, why didn't they do it?"

"They would if they had stayed long enough,"
replied Bart. "The Government called them
back."

"Sure the Government called them back,"
said Rabig with a sardonic grin. "It got cold
feet. It saw that Mexico wasn't going to back
down, and so it backed down itself. Now if
Germany had started out to catch Villa, it would
have caught him."

"Now cut that out, Rabig," said Frank sharply. "If the President called the soldiers back, he had good reason for doing it. He knows a good deal more about what is going on than the rest of us do. He probably knew that Germany would like nothing better than to see us get mixed up in a row with Mexico and have to keep our troops on this side of the water instead of sending them over to Europe. He wasn't going to play Germany's game, and that's the reason he let up on Villa, who doesn't amount to anything anyway."

"That sounds good," returned Rabig, "but it doesn't go with me. The Americans got scared when they saw that the Mexicans meant business. Swell chance the United States would have with Germany when it can't even lick Mexico. These national guard fellows aren't fighters. They're only tin soldiers anyway."

"Tell that to Billy Waldon when he gets back and he'll make you eat your words," said Bart hotly.

"He will, eh?" retorted Rabig. "Just let him try it on, that's all."

"What are you anyway, Rabig, a German or an American?" demanded Frank.

"I was born here and I suppose I'm an American," responded Rabig. "But I couldn't help that and I'm not proud of it."

"And you can bet that America isn't proud of having you born here," said Frank scornfully. "I tell you straight, Rabig, that it won't be healthy for you to keep up that line of talk much longer."

"I don't see any one here that's going to make me stop it," sneered the bully. "Perhaps you'd like to try it."

Frank's eyes flashed and his fist clenched until the knuckles were white. Another instant and that fist would have wiped the sneer from Rabig's face. But the image of his mother rose before him, and by a mighty effort he controlled himself.

"You'll make that bluff once too often some day, Rabig," he said in an even tone.

"Well, if it's a bluff why don't you call it?" sneered Rabig truculently.

Just at this moment Reddy ran up to them, considerably excited.

"Mr. Sheldon!" he exclaimed, addressing himself to Frank, "Oliver Twist has climbed up the water pipe at the end of the building and now the pipe's broke and he can't get down."

Oliver Twist was the office cat, who had gained his name because, like the hero in Dickens' famous story, he was continually "asking for more." He was a favorite with all except Rabig, who kicked at him whenever he got in his way. So that the news of his plight aroused instant interest and sympathy, and all flocked to the window that Reddy indicated.

There was Oliver, sure enough, a thoroughly frightened cat, and with good reason.

The building was five stories high and a leader pipe ran at one end of it from the top nearly to the ground. There was a sparrow's nest up near the eaves, and Oliver had evidently been tempted to make it a visit. But a section of the pipe about two-thirds of the way up had rotted and under the cat's weight had broken off. Oliver with a cat's quickness had saved himself by clutching at a metal ring that encircled the pipe just above the broken part and had swung himself up out of immediate danger.

But although safe for the moment, he had no way of escape. He was more than three stories from the ground and if he let go would be killed or maimed. If he climbed farther up he would be no better off, for the projecting roof of the building made it impossible to leap to it.

Oliver was in a bad fix, and his piteous mews as he clung to the pipe showed that he realized it. All his nine lives were in imminent danger. It would not have been so bad if he had had a ledge or projection to rest on until he could be rescued. But this was lacking, with the exception of the narrow ring less than an inch wide that encircled the pipe, and though his claws dug desperately against this it was certain that his strength would not enable him to maintain himself long in this position.

There was a chorus of exclamations and suggestions from the young men who crowded the window.

"Let's get a rope and a basket and let it down from the roof," suggested Tom Bradford.

"That wouldn't do," objected Hal. "He'd be too frightened to get into it. He wouldn't let go his grip on the pipe."

"Somebody get a ladder," cried Reddy.

"We haven't one that would be long enough to reach him," said Bart.

Frank's keen eyes and alert mind had been judging the situation. Now he spoke.

"We can get him from that window, fellows," he said pointing to a window about six feet above the cat and a little to one side.

"I don't know," said Bart, dubiously, as he eyed the window. "Seems to me like a forlorn hope. A fellow would have to have the arms of a gorilla to reach the cat from there."

"Never mind about that," responded Frank. "Let's get up there quick and I'll show you what I have in mind."

The crowd raced pell-mell up the stairs and then through an old storeroom on the upper floor until they reached the window.

It had not been opened all winter, and had been so warped by sleet and snow that it yielded to the pressure of their arms groaningly and reluctantly. But at last, just when they were about ready to give up, they accomplished the feat and looked out.

Oliver saw them and hailed them evidently as his last hope, for he broke into a storm of wails.

"There," said Bart, regretfully. "I told you we'd be too far off to do him any good."

He leaned out as far as he could without danger of falling, and the cat was still three feet at least from the tips of his outstretched fingers.

"Nothing doing," he ejaculated as he withdrew from his vain effort.

"There's just one chance," said Frank. "One of us fellows will have to hang out there head downward, his full length, while the rest grab him by the legs and hold on for dear life."

"That sounds easy if you say it quick," cut in Reddy. "But who's going to be the goat?"

"I am," said Frank, as he threw off his coat.

"Oh come now, Frank!" expostulated Tom. "That's taking too big a risk. I hate to see the poor brute go down, but his life isn't worth yours."

"Besides," put in Bart, "even if you got hold of Oliver he'd probably be so frightened that he'd claw your head off."

"Cut out the talk, fellows," said Frank. "Bart, you and Tom hold on to one leg while Reddy and Hal grab the other."

Two others of the group, Will Baxter and Dick Ormsby, joined the quartette of helpers, although with considerable inward quaking, for they felt that if anything happened to their comrade they would be in part responsible for not having forcibly detained him from such a risky undertaking.

A moment more and Frank had lowered himself outside of the sill and hung at full length, while three strong pairs of arms clutched at each leg. He found himself on a level with the cat but too far to one side to reach him with his extended hand.

"Start swinging, fellows!" he called out, "until I'm able to reach him."

They swayed him gently to and fro, each time bringing him a few inches nearer to the cat, whose strength was rapidly giving way and who seemed to be slipping.

Frank made one grab and missed. His next attempt, however, was more fortunate. He gripped the cat by the neck and shoulders, gave a wrench and pulled him away from the pipe.

The frightened brute, seeing only open space below him, writhed and twisted about frantically, but Frank held him tight despite his clawings, and in another moment the six above had pulled him up to and over the sill, where he dropped on the floor, panting and breathless.

Oliver, released, flew round and round the room, until his excitement subsided and he curled up in a corner, his sides heaving, and his eyes still big and wild from the fright of his late experience.

"And the cat came back!" chanted Reddy.

"The main thing is that Frank came back," said Bart. "I tell you what, old boy, that was a nervy thing to do."

"There isn't another fellow in the place who would have done it," said Hal. "My heart was in my mouth while he was swinging there head down. Once I was so scared I almost let go."

"It's lucky for everybody but the undertaker that you didn't," said Frank with a grin, as he dusted his clothes and arranged his collar and tie. "I don't mind admitting myself that the ground looked awful far away while I was swinging there."

"You're in luck to come out of it with a good pair of eyes," said Bart. "If Oliver's claws had once got to them there would have been something doing."

"Well now let's get back downstairs," said Frank, leading the way, while Reddy brought up the rear with the recovered and somewhat chastened Oliver perched upon his shoulder.

It would be safe to say that for some time to come sparrows' nests, especially if located near leader pipes, would have no further attractions. For once Oliver Twist would not ask for more!

finish

CHAPTER IV

WAR

As the crowd of young fellows came trooping into the office, old Peterson, who alone had kept at his books, looked up with a reproof upon his lips.

"What do you fellows think this is, a business office or an athletic club?" he demanded.

But the querulous look and tone vanished when he had heard the story of Oliver's rescue, and as he turned to his books again the old veteran of many battlefields muttered to himself:

"The old American stuff is in the boys yet. If he's the kind that Uncle Sam is going to send to the trenches, Heaven help the Kaiser!"

Three weeks went by, weeks of stern resolve and feverish expectation. It was becoming evident now to every mind that America could not, if she would, keep out of the war except at the expense of national honor.

Every day brought it's toll of sinking ships and murdered crews, of wanton brutality and flagrant disregard of plighted faith. The whole world was sickening of the German name.

The city of Camport felt the quickening thrill that was running through the continent from coast to coast. War was the universal topic. In the shop, in the street, in the church, in the courthouse, the one prevailing subject was war.

The mad dog of Europe was running wild, and it was up to America to join with all the rest of the civilized world in putting an end to his depredations.

The Thirty-seventh had come back to Camport from the Mexican border, the men hard as nails, sound as nuts, brown as berries, eager and ardent for the tremendous task before them, and as the regiment swung through the streets, headed by the band, keeping step to the strain of martial airs, the little city went wild with enthusiasm.

"There's no use, Frank," said Bart, as with the other young fellows of the place they thronged the windows to see the regiment go by. "I'm going to join."

"Same here," said Frank. "I can feel Uncle Sam's hand on my shoulder this minute."

"We're coming father Abraham, one hundred thousand strong!" sang out Reddy, from his place on a stool behind them where he had perched himself so as to be able to look over their heads.

Just then Billy Waldon passed in the ranks and looked up at them with a cheerful grin.

"There's Billy!" cried Tom. "Oh, boy! wouldn't I like to be marching alongside of him!"

"Let's go around to the armory this very night, Frank, and give in our names!" cried Bart. "I tell you, this thing's got me, got me bad."

"It's got me just as bad," said Frank, "and the only question is, in just what branch of the service I'm going to enlist when the President calls for troops. I want to see action and see it quick, and I have the idea that perhaps the regular army boys will get into the trenches sooner than the national guard. I'll talk it over with my mother to-day and then I'll decide."

By the time the noon hour arrived the parade was over, and Frank, with his heart and mind full of the stirring scenes he had witnessed, went home to lunch.

It was only when the modest little house came into view that his thoughts took a more sober turn and his step slowed a little. Up to now he had been thinking chiefly of himself. He was like a hound straining at the leash. Every instinct in him clamored to be in the very thick and front of the coming fight.

But there was his mother, his mother, whose eyes had grown larger and more wistful of late as every day had brought nearer and nearer the conflict that was about to claim her only son. He was all that she had, her one strong support and sure refuge and loving comrade.

What would she do, alone and anguished in this quiet home while he was battling at the front in a rain of shells, of poison gas, of liquid fire?

But he must not sadden her by carrying into the house this shadow of coming events that for the moment had flung itself over him, and he assumed a gaiety that he did not feel as he ran lightly up the steps where she, as usual, stood waiting for him in the open door.

She on her part had hidden her heartache beneath a mask of vivacity. It was a loving deception where each knew that the other was trying to deceive and failing in the attempt.

"Well," she asked, cheerily, as they sat down to the tasteful meal she had prepared for him, "what is the news in the city to-day? It seems to me that I have heard nothing but band music all morning."

"I guess the band didn't leave anything out," said Frank with a smile. "They played through the whole list of national airs from the "Star Spangled Banner" to "Dixie."

"But I heard something else too," went on his mother. "What was it the newsboys were crying through the streets?"

"Oh it was an extra of some kind," said Frank, evasively.

"But of what kind?" asked his mother with a gentle persistence.

"Why, it was about the President's speech," said Frank, reluctantly. "He's expected to address the Senate this afternoon, and everybody is eager to know what he will have to say."

"I can guess what it will be," said his mother, sadly.

"Yes," agreed Frank, "There's no use blinking the facts, little Mother. He's going to declare that the United States is at war with Germany. And high time, too!" he burst out, his pent-up convictions finding voice. "We've been patient, Mother, till patience becomes a fault. We've waited and hoped and written and argued, and all the while Germany has been growing more vile and brutal. Any further patience would be cowardice. And that's one thing that, with all its faults, our country has never been guilty of. It's up to us now, Mother, every one of us," and he emphasized the words, "to show that we're worthy to be called Americans."

"Yes," faltered his mother, "I suppose it

is—in my heart I know it is. But oh, my boy! my boy! how can I let you go?"

"It's duty, Mother," said Frank, gently. "It isn't a question of choice. I *must* go. My country needs me, and I know my mother well enough to be sure she would be the last one in the world to hold me back."

Before his mother could reply there was a commotion in the street outside. They looked at each other inquiringly and then rose from the table and hurried to the window.

Most of the houses in Camport had been decorated with Old Glory in honor of the return of the favorite regiment. Frank had seen to it early in the morning that his own flag had swung from a pole set in the upper window.

Through the whole length of the street there was not a house that did not show from some point of vantage the Stars and Stripes.

The house directly opposite Frank's had gone even further. Upon one of the pillars of the porch had been deftly grouped the flags of France and England with Old Glory in the center. It was a type of the alliance that bound together or was soon to bind three of the great nations that were to fight side by side the battle of civilization against barbarism.

Before the house where these emblems were

displayed, a little knot of people were arguing and gesticulating. One of them, a burly fellow, had a face that bore the German stamp. He was greatly excited and his arms were waving like windmills as he pointed at the three flags that seemed to have stirred him to anger.

Suddenly, in a fit of rage, he broke away from the group, ran up the walk to the house, grabbed the offending colors from the pillar of the porch and threw them to the ground where he stamped upon them.

Mrs. Sheldon gasped.

With a bound Frank reached the door, flung it open and rushed across the street. The fellow who had vented his rage on the flags looked up. He saw Frank coming, and the sight of that flying figure, with taut muscles and blazing eyes was not reassuring.

He ran down the walk in an effort to escape. Frank met him at the gate. Like a flash Frank's fist shot out and the vandal measured his length on the ground.

CHAPTER V

A VANDAL PUNISHED

A CROWD rose magically from nowhere. People came running, shouting, jostling, demanding an explanation from their neighbors, who, in turn, demanded it of them.

"It's Frank Sheldon!" shouted someone, above the uproar.

"He's making hash of a Hun!" yelled another. "Come on and see the show, fellows— admission free!"

Through all this confusion, Bart, who had been on his way back to the office when attracted by the hubbub, pushed and elbowed his way through to the first line of observers.

"What's the row, Frank?" he yelled. "Stop kneeling on that fellow's neck and tell us about it. Look out!" as the fellow made a quick move as though to wrench himself free from Frank's grasp. "Don't let him put one over on you."

"Don't worry!" Frank's face was grim as he rose to his feet dragging the now thoroughly cowed German after him. "There's not a Hun

37

in this country or the old that'll be able to get away from me once I get my hands on him—not after this day's work. Do you know what he did?" He gave his captive a ferocious shake and glared about at the still-increasing mob. "Do you know what this yellow dog did, right here in the country that's made him?"

"No, give it to us," shouted someone in the crowd, and the rest took it up impatiently.

"Yes, give it to us, Sheldon," they cried. "Get to the point!"

"Look at those flags," Frank cried in answer, pointing with quivering finger to the sullied emblems that lay in the dust where the German had left them. "Those are the flags of liberty, justice and right, and this dog," his fingers tightened in the man's collar till the craven cried out with the pain of it, "dragged them down, threw them in the dust, stamped upon them—stamped upon them, fellows! And our flag, Old Glory, is among them! Do you hear that? Old Glory is among them!"

An ominous growl went up from the crowd which had been listening breathlessly and with growing indignation to Frank's words, and now it surged threateningly forward.

"What are we going to do with him?" cried Frank, his eyes afire. "What would you do with a cur like this?"

"Tar and feather him!" cried someone, and a score of voices took it up.

"Tar and feather him! tar and feather him!"

"Ride him out of town on a rail!"

"Aw, that's too easy," yelled another, making a megaphone of his hands so that his voice soared above even that deafening babel. "I've got a good tough rope, fellows, tough enough even for this hog here. What do you say?"

"Lynch him! lynch him!" the cry arose deafeningly and the crowd surged forward once more closing in upon Frank and his quivering, terrified captive.

"Out of the way, Sheldon!"

"Let's get at him!"

"Oh, mein Gott!" wailed the German, sinking on his knees and gazing up at Frank with terror-stricken face. "You will not let dem murder me—like dis—in gold blood—you will not—"

"There's not much cold blood about this," said Frank, with a glint in his eye and another tightening of his fingers. "However, we'll let you live a little while yet. You're not fit to die."

"Lynch him! lynch him!" the cry still rose menacingly. The crowd was becoming impatient.

"Wait a minute;" shouted Frank, straightening himself to his full height and holding up his hand compellingly. "We're not going to lynch this man. We're going to punish him worse than that."

The German's face, which had grown hopeful at the beginning of Frank's speech, resumed its terrified expression and he sank back despairingly.

The shouts and cries of the crowd had settled down now to a muttering, murmuring, undertone so that Frank's voice rose clear and determined above it.

"First of all," he said, while the crowd surged forward in mingled disappointment and eagerness, "he's going to pick up the flags he has dared insult, dust them off carefully and restore them to their former position."

The crowd shouted its delight at the suggestion, while the German's face grew sullen and he looked stolidly at the ground.

"I vill not do it," he muttered.

"What's that?" queried Frank politely, while his knuckles dug deep into his captive's neck. "I'm afraid I didn't quite understand you. If you will repeat—"

"I said I vould not do it," cried the German, with a sudden flare up of his old rage and hatred. "Und vat I say I mean."

"But I'm sure you will change your mind,"

Frank answered still gently, while the crowd watched eagerly. "Within the next minute I am almost sure you are going to pick up the flags, dust them off neatly and put them back where you found them. If a little pressure is needed, why, I am always willing to oblige."

A sharp twist of the collar he held brought a guttural cry of pain from the Prussian and a crow of delight from the crowd.

"More yet?" queried Frank with another twist that brought the man to his knees whimpering. "Or will you do what I suggested?"

"I will do it," growled the German, hatred and pain in the glance he flung his captor. "Led me go und I vill do it."

"Good," said Frank. "I'll let you do it but I won't let you go. I love you too much. Right this way."

The crowd gave way before the advance of captor and captive, and before them all the German was forced to pick up the flags, dust them to the entire satisfaction of his gleeful audience, and, with Frank's knuckles still urging him on, replace them to the best of his clumsy ability as he had found them.

With the flags of the triple alliance floating once more proudly in the breeze, the throng sent up a mighty shout. Hats were thrown in the air and cries were heard.

"That's Old Glory for you! The more they try to down her the higher up she flies!"

"That's what the whole German nation's going to do when we get our boys over there!"

"We'll make 'em tremble in their boots!"

"And now," cried Frank, "our German friend will stand at salute and sing the Star Spangled Banner with all the expression I know his love for our country will prompt."

The German balked again but under the same gentle pressure as before sang in husky tones and guttural accents the stirring measures of our national hymn.

"And last of all," shouted Frank, while the throng, wild with delight, surged forward once more, "our dear enemy will, with all the reverence due the greatest flag in the world, kneel here in the dust and kiss the Stars and Stripes. Now then, kneel."

"I vill not," cried the German, trying to wrench himself free. "You cannot force me—"

"We'll see about that," said Frank, while the crowd grew threatening once more. "Will you do it—or shall I make you?"

"I will not do it," the Prussian reiterated stubbornly. "I have done all the rest but dat I vill not."

"Kiss the flag," cried Frank, now thoroughly aroused, his knuckles showing white as they gripped his captive's collar. "Come on—we're waiting."

Slowly and relentlessly he forced the German to his knees, and driven by pain and fear of the mob his captive finally touched his lips to the flag.

"And now," cried Frank, flinging the Prussian from him and dusting off his hands as though they were polluted, "make yourself scarce. But remember after this to respect the American flag. Americans are behind it!"

The crowd pushed and jostled the disheveled vandal as he slunk away and then, after cheering Frank, gradually dispersed.

"Boy, it was neat work!" cried Bart, as the two friends crossed the street together. "Coming on to the office?"

"No, I've got to see mother first and straighten my tie," grinned Frank. "I'll probably catch up to you though. So long."

Frank found his mother awaiting him with outstretched arms.

"Oh, my boy," she cried, "you were splendid! If you will wait just a little while till our affairs are more settled I will not say a word to your joining the army. If all Germans are like that—"

"They are, Mother," replied Frank, grimly. "Germany is a nation of men like him. What he did to our flags the whole Prussian empire is trying to do to the world."

"Then you must go!" cried his mother, holding him from her and regarding him with flaming eyes. "Because I love my son, I will give him—for my dear France and for America!"

CHAPTER VI

THE DIE IS CAST

"That's it, Mother," cried Frank, his whole soul responding to the kindling spirit in her eyes. "For America and France, the two greatest republics in the world. It won't be the first time they've fought together."

"No," replied his mother proudly. "Lafayette and other brave sons of France helped this country to win its independence, and it is only right that now when France is hard pressed and pouring out her blood like water, Americans should fight side by side with her to make the world safe for democracy."

"You're a true daughter of France, Mother," said Frank, admiringly.

"Ah, *la belle* France," sighed his mother. "I love her with all my heart and soul. How many times I have longed to go back and see her sunny vineyards and her beautiful cities."

"You and father were planning to go over there just before the war broke out, weren't you, Mother?" asked Frank.

"Yes," replied Mrs. Sheldon. "And for two

reasons. I was wild to see the dear homeland again, and then, too, I felt I ought to go to see about the property my father, your grandfather, left me. But then your dear father died, and after that I had no heart to go. Nor could I have gone anyway, had I wished, for the war would have made it almost impossible."

"Well, we don't care much for the property, Mother," said Frank. "While I've got two strong arms I'll support you. And yet," he added, a little more thoughtfully, "it wouldn't have been a bad thing if we had been able to sell it so that you could have the money now when I am liable to be called away. We've got only this house and the little money that dad left us, and I'm afraid you will have all you can do to get along."

"Don't worry about me," replied the mother in a tone that strove to be cheerful. "You know I have the true French thrift—you've said yourself that I am a wonderful manager—I can make a little money go a long way. The only reason I ever cared for the property was for your sake, so that you could get a good start in the world. I don't know now that we can ever get it. It was tangled up in a lawsuit and that was one of the reasons why I ought to have been there in person when the estate was being settled."

"Never mind, little Mother," cried Frank gaily, "I'm the richest fellow in the world this minute with such a mother as you are."

He gave her a quick embrace and kiss and hurried out of the house, for he had been away from the office considerably longer than usual. But quick as was the time he made in getting downtown, the news of his exploit had preceded him and he found the place buzzing with excitement.

Bart, who had let the story lose nothing in the telling, gave him a resounding thump on the back as he came in.

"Here's the fellow that made the Hun eat crow," he cried, jubilantly.

"And from all accounts it didn't agree with him," grinned Tom. "It was a dandy bit of work, Frank. I only wish I'd been there to see you make the Hun kiss the flag."

"Bully for you, old scout!" cried Hal. "There's a lot of other fellows in this town that ought to get the same treatment. I know some of them that had a regular party the day the news came that the *Lusitania* was sunk."

"I heard of that, too," said Frank. "But we want to remember, fellows, that not all Germans felt that way. Some of them felt just as shocked and outraged over it as we did ourselves. There are lots of fellows with German blood in their veins that are just as good Americans as we are."

"I suppose there are," conceded Bart, a little grudgingly. "Not all of them are tarred with the same brush. But there are too many of them who regard Germany as their father and America as their father-in-law, and you know which one of the two a fellow is apt to like better."

Just then Rabig passed through the room on his way to another part of the building. He cast a sour look upon the group, and there was special malignity in his gaze as it rested for a moment on Frank.

"You're about as popular with Rabig as a rattlesnake is with a picnic party," laughed Bart, as Rabig went on. "If looks could kill you'd be a dead man this minute. He hated you before, but he hates you worse now since he's heard of that little fracas. Gee, how I'd like to see him have to kneel and kiss the flag!"

"He'd try to bite it," put in Reddy.

At this moment a group of newsboys passed outside, shouting their extras.

"I guess that means the President's gone and done it," cried Frank. "Here, Reddy, take this dime and go out and get one of those papers. If you're back in half a minute you can keep the change."

"Whoop-ee!" cried Reddy, and was off like a bullet from a gun. Soon he was back with the coveted paper, still damp from the press.

Across the top in screaming headlines was the phrase:

President Declares War on Germany!

"That settles it," said Frank. "We're in for it, now."

"Up to the neck," put in Reddy, whose small frame held an unlimited amount of patriotism. "Gee, I wish I was old enough to get in it. I wouldn't wait for no draft!"

"And now that we're in, we're in for keeps. That's America's way," said Bart.

"She's put her hand to the plow and she won't turn back," said old Peterson, solemnly, and into his dim eyes came the light that had shone there when, in his youth, he had stormed with his regiment the heights of Lookout Mountain.

There was little more work done in the office that day. Business, for the time, seemed a trivial thing. Something far greater and nobler filled the hearts of these ardent young Americans.

They heard the tramp of marching multitudes, they saw their country's flag unfurled, those glorious Stars and Stripes, that had never been smirched with dishonor, or gone down in

defeat. And in their hearts they swore that
what had been true in the past should be true,
too, in the future, though they might shed their
blood and lose their lives in making it true.

A great mass meeting was organized that
night and Bart and Frank attended it. The
hall was thronged, and eloquent speakers voiced
the feeling that filled the hearts of all. But
nothing stirred them so strongly as when the
final orator closed his speech with a scathing
denunciation of the Prussian foe, quoted from
one of America's noblest sons:

"They have gone forth to battle in the
spirit of their ancestral Huns. Wreckers of
cathedrals, destroyers of libraries, despoilers
of cemeteries, slayers of old men and women
and children, barbarians by instinct, pirates and
incendiaries by practice, terrorists by training,
slaves by habit and bullies by profession—maim-
ing, poisoning, burning, suffocating, deporting,
enslaving, murderers of the very souls of a
people so far as it is in their power—the rest
of the world can live on terms of peace and
good will with them only after they have
drained to the dregs the bitter cup of military
defeat!"

Thunders of applause swept through the hall
as the speaker finished.

"Say, but that was a rattling speech," remarked Bart, as the two chums walked home together.

"Yes," agreed Frank, "it was magnificent. But after all, Bart, it will take more than words to win this war. It's up to us to turn those words into deeds. It's bullets and bayonets that count!"

finish

CHAPTER VII

FOR LOVE OF COUNTRY

ALTHOUGH it was nearly midnight when he reached home, Frank found his mother sitting up and waiting for him.

"You shouldn't have sat up for me, Mother," he said, in tones of tender reproach. "It's too bad that you should be robbed of your sleep like this."

"I don't mind as long as I know you're coming," replied his mother. "It is the other nights I shall dread, the nights when I shall not hear your footsteps on the porch, and I'm afraid that time is coming very soon."

"I fear it is, Mother," he replied gently. "There's only one thing left for me to do. I have felt it before, but I feel it more than ever after what I've heard to-night. I wish you'd been there, Mother, and heard the unbelievable things I did about the way the Germans are carrying on this war. And yet again I'm glad you weren't, for it would have turned your very soul sick. There's no use talking, the Prussian spirit must be crushed, and until it is, this world won't be a fit place to live in."

52

"I know you are right, dear," responded Mrs. Sheldon. "And though it breaks my heart to have you go, I'll give you up as cheerfully as I can and try to live through the long days when you're away from me. Of one thing I feel sure, that wherever you go, or whatever your country calls upon you to do, you'll make me proud of you."

"I'll do my best, Mother," Frank replied. "I'm not going for glory or for promotion or anything else except to see my country win the war. All I ask is a chance to do my bit."

Camport was a changed city the next day. A new spirit and new purpose were visible in the looks of all. The long strain of waiting was over and America was girding herself for the fight.

"Well," old Peterson was saying as Frank entered the office, "it's up to you young fellows to show that America's still got the stuff. I only wish I were young enough to shoulder a gun and go myself."

"You've done your share, Mr. Peterson," said Bart. "If the boys of to-day do as well as those who wore the blue and gray they'll show the Prussians where they get off."

"It will make a big change in this place," said the old bookkeeper, as he looked around at the group of eager faces. "You young roosters all seem to be aching to get into the scrap, and there won't be any of you left."

"Rabig will be here," piped up Reddy, and there was a general laugh.

"I could spare him," growled old Peterson, with whom Rabig was about as unpopular as he was with the younger men.

"Well, fellows, let's count noses," said Frank. "How many of us are going to enlist and how many of us are going to wait for the draft?"

"Enlist! enlist!" came in a general chorus, reinforced by Reddy's shrill treble.

"You'll have to wait awhile, Reddy," laughed Frank. "Your heart's all right, but Uncle Sam isn't ready for the kids yet."

"Mr. Peterson said there were boys in the Union army only fourteen years old," grumbled Reddy. "And if they could fight I don't see why I can't."

"I'm going into the navy," announced Dick Ormsby, whose father was a retired sea captain. "I've got the love of blue water in my veins I guess, and I'm aching to get a chance to pot a German U-boat."

"Me for the aviators!" cried Will Baxter. "I always wanted to be a high flyer—now I've got the chance. I know all about running a motorcycle and that ought to help a lot."

"I'd like to join the cavalry," joined in Hal

Chase. "But they don't seem to have much use for them in this war. Horses can't go over trenches and barbed wire fences."

"The infantry's good enough for me," declared Frank.

"And for me, too," echoed Bart. "Uncle Sam needs men in every branch, but after all, it's the hand to hand fighting of the armies that's going to decide this war."

At this moment, Mr. Moore, the senior member of the firm, came out from his office. He was a large man with a genial face and bearing, and was generally liked by his employees to whom he was fair and just.

His eyes twinkled as he saw the alacrity with which the young men scattered to their desks.

"Don't worry, boys," he said. "I know that your minds aren't much on business to-day, and I don't wonder. To tell the truth, I'd be sorry if they were. There come times when there's only one important thing in the world, and this is one of the times. I've got just a word to say to you boys," he went on. "I don't know just what each one of you is planning to do in connection with this war. Each one of you must decide that matter for himself. From things I've heard, most of you seem eager to go. I shall be sorry to lose you, for we never were busier than we are now, but I should be still more sorry to have you stay here when your country needs you at the front.

"Mr. Thomas and I have been talking this thing over and we want to say to you that as far as the money part of it is concerned you needn't hesitate. We're not going to let you lose a cent by following your patriotic instinct. Some of you have dependents at home who rely in part or wholly upon what you earn. So we have decided that your salaries will go on as usual—that is, that we will make up the difference between what the Government pays you and what you are getting now. In that way you will be able to serve your country with nothing on your mind except the best and quickest way to win the war."

A spontaneous cheer rose from the young men, as with a smile and wave of his hand their employer turned back to his office.

"Gee, but he's a game sport!" exclaimed Reddy, voicing forcibly if inelegantly the feeling of all.

If there had been any hesitation before, this generous speech removed it and now the boys were ready for action.

That very evening Frank and Bart, accompanied by Billy Waldon, went to the headquarters of the Thirty-seventh regiment. Here they put in their applications for enlistment.

There were few formalities, for the regiment was eager to recruit its numbers up to full strength.

Neither one of the chums had any trouble in passing the physical examination, for both were splendid specimens of manhood. Frank was six feet tall in his stocking feet, straight and lithe as an Indian, and with fine muscular development.

Bart, who was two inches shorter, was broad shouldered, well set up, and capable of great endurance. All the prodding of the doctors failed to reveal the slightest defect, and they passed the test triumphantly.

Then they took the oath of allegiance, promising in words what they had long since promised in their hearts, and were duly enrolled as members of the famous regiment.

"Well, now you're one of us, boys," cried Billy, as he grasped the hand of each warmly. "And, believe me, it's a great old regiment to belong to. Come along and I'll show you some of the flags we carried in the Civil War."

They went with him through the armory and saw some of the treasured relics that the regiment cherished as its most priceless possessions.

There were the old flags, blackened with powder, torn with bullets, that had gone through the fire of Antietam and Gettysburg and Chickamauga.

The boys took off their hats as they stood before them.

There were the cannon that had thundered on the banks of the Rapidan and in the valley of the Shenandoah. A glass case covered a letter of commendation for a wild charge that had saved the day at Shiloh. There was the blood-stained hat of the colonel who had fallen while leading the regiment at Gaines' Mill.

"That was the kind of stuff the regiment was made up of in the old days," said Billy, proudly.

"It's a glorious record," said Frank, reverently. "And now it's up to us to show that what the old boys did in Virginia, the young fellows are going to do again in France!"

CHAPTER VIII

OFF TO CAMP

Now that the momentous step had been taken, the boys buckled down to work—work of the hardest and most strenuous kind.

They left their positions with Moore and Thomas the next day, with the hearty good wishes of the firm and the assurance that their places would be ready for them as soon as they returned.

The only gloomy member of the office force was Tom Bradford, who had also applied for enlistment but had been rejected on account of his teeth. Now he had on a grouch of the grouchiest kind.

"Hang the red tape!" he growled. "What have a fellow's teeth got to do with it? I don't want to bite the Germans, I want to shoot them."

"Never mind, old scout," comforted Bart. "Perhaps the dentist can fix that up. Anyway you can root for us if you can't go along."

"Not much nourishment in that," grunted

Tom, refusing to be shaken from his attitude of settled gloom.

"It does seem mighty hard," remarked Bart, after Tom had left them. "I don't think the Government ought to be so particular. The time may come when they'll be glad enough to get such fine fellows as Tom, teeth or no teeth."

"Perhaps so," agreed Frank; "but just now they've got such a lot of material that they can afford to pick and choose. And after all, perhaps they're right. They've got to have a pretty high level of physical condition."

"I suppose you're right," said Bart, adding: "Suppose poor old Tom should get a toothache in the trenches. You can't expect to have dentists on tap."

"As far as that goes," Frank took him up quickly, grinning at the picture that rose before his mind, "I should think a good hard toothache would be an asset. You'd be so mad you could kill a dozen Germans. It would just be getting your mind off your agony."

Bart grinned.

"Yes and it would have another advantage. When you've got a toothache you don't care whether you live or die. Getting stabbed with a bayonet would be almost a relief."

"That's so," laughed Frank. "He'd be something like the seasick passenger who, for the first hour, was afraid he was going to die and after that was afraid he couldn't. I suppose Uncle Sam figures it this way," he went on, "if a chain has a single weak link in it the whole chain is weak.

"You know how it is in a crowd. A hundred people may be eager to get out of a place, but if two or three in front are slow it holds up the whole hundred. But I'm willing to bet that someway or somehow Tom will manage to get in."

"I hope so, anyway," said Bart. "I'd like to have the old scout along with us."

A day or two later the boys got their uniforms and then they began to feel like genuine soldiers. It set them apart from other men and emphasized the fact that from now on they had but one aim in life, to fight and, if need be, die for Uncle Sam.

The first sight of Frank in khaki was a stab at the mother heart of Mrs. Sheldon, although she could not avoid a thrill of admiration at the splendid figure that he made. To her it meant separation, a separation that was coming swiftly nearer with each passing day. And there might be no reunion!

But, although her lips were tremulous, her eyes were bright and she kept her forebodings bravely under cover. She was a thoroughbred, and it was easy to see where Frank had inherited his spirit.

"How proud your father would be if he could see you now," she said with a slight tremble in her voice, which she strove to conceal.

"Perhaps he does," said Frank reverently. "If he were here I know that he would approve of what I'm doing."

The days were all too short now for the work that was crowded into them. Government preparations were going on with feverish rapidity. Events followed one another as though on wings.

The order had gone forth for the draft and another order had decreed that the regiments of the national guard should be enrolled in and form part of the regular army.

This latter order was the subject of some regret with the members of the old Thirty-seventh, whose pride in their regiment was intense and who had hoped to have it remain intact under its old officers for the period of the war.

"We'll lose our identity now," mourned Billy Waldon. "We'll just be part of some big rainbow division, made up of fellows from all over the United States. For my part, I think it's a mistake. I think the regiment would fight better under its own colors and with its old traditions to inspire it."

"We mustn't criticize the Government, Billy," said Frank. "My theory all through this war is going to be that Uncle Sam is right. He's got good reasons for everything he does."

"'Them's my sentiments'," put in Bart. "Whether we have the regimental colors or not, we'll all be fighting under the one flag, Old Glory, and it's only the Stars and Stripes that counts, after all. To me there's an inspiration in the thought of the whole United States, from the Atlantic to the Pacific, fighting as a unit."

"Well, perhaps you're right," said Billy, somewhat mollified. "At any rate, nothing can take away from us the fact that we're volunteers."

A few days passed, then orders came that the regiment should be assembled at the armory to be kept there day and night until they should be sent to Camp Boone—as we shall call the cantonment that had been prepared for them.

To Frank's mother the order sounded like the knell of doom. It was the final step of separation. The word had passed that the boys were to bring all their belongings to the armory as no leave would be given under any circumstances.

"Good-bye, dear boy!" she began bravely, and then all her courage gave way to a storm of tears.

Frank's own eyes were wet as he folded her closely to him and comforted her as best he could, though feeling very much in need of comfort himself.

"Bear up, Mother," he urged. "It will only be a little while before I come marching home again, and I'll be thinking of you all the time and write to you whenever I get a chance."

He forced himself to go at last with many a backward look and wave of his hand at the figure in the doorway. His heart was heavy as he reflected that in the chances of war he might never see her again.

The next few days were full of excitement, allowing him little time to brood. Both he and Bart took to a soldier's life as a duck takes to water. The martial spirit was there together with the quick intelligence that enables America to turn out finished soldiers more quickly than any other country in the world.

They had an advantage too in being sandwiched in, as it were, with the men who had just come back from the Mexican border and had had such recent experience in practical outdoor preparation for fighting.

Billy Waldon, especially, was a mine of information and suggestion, and as they threw themselves into the work with all their heart and soul it was not long before they could feel that they were graduating from the "rookie" class and becoming regular soldiers.

Their commanding officers looked on them

with approval and secretly wished that all of their recruits might be of the same high-class type.

"You're going along like a house afire, fellows," said Billy, after drill had ended one morning. "The manual of arms is just pie for you. Kitchener used to think that it took a year to turn out a soldier. I'll bet if he'd been on this side of the water he'd have felt differently.

"I'm glad you think so," said Frank. "But after all, we're just going through the motions now. The test will come a little later on."

"I'd bet on you now or any time," answered Billy.

The looked-for orders came at last from Washington, and there was a great stir and bustle at the armory. Then the next morning the great doors swung open and the regiment marched forth, headed by its band.

Through the old familiar streets it marched, amid the cheers and tears of those who packed the sidewalks, past the commercial house of Moore and Thomas, where old Peterson waved his hand tremulously and Reddy, with Oliver Twist perched upon his shoulder, shouted himself hoarse and nearly fell out of the window in his enthusiasm, down to the railroad station where the long train waited for them.

There they broke ranks while friends and relatives, fathers and mothers, sisters and broth-

ers, sweethearts and wives, crowded around
them, pressing last gifts into their hands, caress-
ing them, enthusing them, crying over them,
until the warning whistle blew and they were
forced to tear themselves away.

Those few moments had been precious ones
to Frank and his mother, for in them they had
compressed a world of affection, that fell from
their lips and looked from their eyes.

"I won't say good-bye, little Mother," said
Frank. "It's just *au revoir.*"

"Yes, dear," agreed his mother tremulously.
"*Au revoir.* What is that?" she interrupted
herself with a start. "Ah, it is the whistle.
My boy, my boy, I cannot let you go. Yes, I
will be brave," Frank turned his head aside to
hide his own emotion as his mother pathetically
tried to smile. "There, go, dear, go,—before
my resolution breaks entirely. *Au revoir*—my
boy—my boy—"

With a little strangled sound in his throat
Frank tore himself away and, without trusting
himself to look back, climbed into the car with
his jostling comrades. Then he leaned far out
of the window, caught his mother to him and
kissed her.

The whistle shrieked again, and amid a
storm of cheers and waving of handkerchiefs
the train moved out. The old Thirty-seventh
had started on the road to victory!

CHAPTER IX

A NEW LIFE

For some time after the train had started the spirits of the men were subdued. All were thinking of the dear ones they had left behind and might never see again. They were thinking too of the new life—or was it, perhaps, death?—that they were facing.

But it was not in the nature of things that this feeling should long persist amid such a buoyant, boisterous gathering of young fellows and before long the cars of the train were resounding with jests and laughter.

"How far off is this Camp Boone?" asked Bart, who had secured a seat at Frank's side.

"I haven't exactly figured it out," replied the latter, as he stretched his long legs comfortably, "but in the rough, it's about three hundred miles. The way the tracks are crowded now, I don't think we'll get there much before to-morrow morning."

"I don't suppose they'll have it half ready for us," continued Bart. "The Government's had to put it up in an awful hurry."

"We can't expect to find all the comforts of home," returned Frank. "But as long as we have a place to sleep and three square meals a day I guess there won't be much kick coming."

"There will be no discount on the grub," put in Billy Waldon. "Uncle Sam's a good provider and he'll see that his boys have plenty to eat."

Frank's prediction was fulfilled, for it was early the next morning when the train stopped at the little town from which Camp Boone was about three miles distant.

It was a glorious morning for a hike and after the commissary department had done its duty and each man had tucked away a good breakfast under his belt the regiment fell into line and covered the intervening miles in quick time. All were filled with eagerness to see the place that was to be their home during many months of training.

It was a busy scene that met their eyes when at last they came within view of the camp. A small army of workmen was swarming all over the place and the sounds of hammers and groaning of derricks and hum of machinery filled the air with a deafening din.

"Didn't I tell you it would be only half finished?" said Bart. "I hope they've got roofs on the barracks. They say they have bad weather around here and I don't want to get killed before I meet a German. Gee, that would be tough luck!"

"You can't build a city in a single night," Frank replied, as he saw the apparently endless row of buildings prepared for their reception. "And that's what this is going to be—a city in itself. The wonder to me is, not that they've done so little but that they've done so much."

"They say there are going to be thirty thousand soldiers here," put in Billy Waldon. "Before a month is over there'll be more fellows living here than people in the whole city of Camport. That gives you some idea of the work the Government has to do. But Uncle Sam is some worker when he once takes his coat off. Even the Kaiser will admit that before he gets through with him."

The regiment had filed through the great gate in perfect order, but once inside, the officers quickly gave the command to break ranks, for they themselves were quite as eager as the men to inspect their new quarters.

The camp had been skillfully laid out by one of the most distinguished architects in the country. It's general form was that of the letter U about two miles long and a mile in width. The ground was slightly rolling and had been nearly cleared of trees in order to permit the erection of the buildings.

But the architect had not sacrificed everything to mere utility for in one corner of the camp a large grove of noble trees had been left untouched and took away from the bareness of the general plan.

Along the sides of the camp stretched the barracks, plain, two-story frame buildings hastily put together and guiltless of any attempt at decoration.

On the floors were endless rows of cots with just enough space left to afford a passage between them. There were no heating arrangements as yet, but, as summer was just beginning, this was a matter of no importance and there would be ample time for that later on.

There were separate buildings that served as mess halls for the various regiments. The officers' buildings were grouped together in a special section and these, although plain, were a little more elaborate than those destined for the men.

Besides these there was a host of other buildings, stables for the horses, laundries, lavatories, shower baths and all the other structures that were essential to a city that had sprung up like Jonah's gourd, almost over night.

"Not half bad, eh, old man?" said Bart, giving his chum a bang on the shoulder.

"I should say not," replied Frank. "They

don't seem to have forgotten much. It's neat but not gaudy."

"Now if our friend, the chef, is all right," grinned Bart, "and isn't stingy with the grub, we'll have nothing left to ask for."

"We'll get a line on that pretty soon, I hope," said Frank, his eyes wandering wistfully in the direction of the mess tent. "That hike's made me hungry enough to eat nails. When the mess horn toots you won't be able to see me, I'll run so fast."

"I'll race you," said Bart. "Mother used to say I had the appetite of a wolf. Now I feel like a pack of 'em."

Any misgivings that they might have had on that subject were promptly dispelled by their first meal in camp. The food served was well cooked and abundant and those who sought a second or even a third helping were not denied.

"Well," remarked Bart, with a sigh born of comfort and repletion as he rose from the meal, "I guess Napoleon was right when he said that an army travels on its stomach."

"Gee, if that's so, Uncle Sam's boys will travel some distance," said Billy Waldon with a grin.

"As far as Berlin, you bet!" cried Frank emphatically.

Before many days had passed the regiment

had fully settled down into the routine of army life at Camp Boone.

That routine was almost unvarying and therein lay its value in molding the growing army into a perfect fighting machine. It fostered team work of the finest kind.

At six o'clock the bugle blew reveille that called the sleepers from their cots. There was no disregarding that imperative summons, no turning over for another "forty winks."

In an instant the sleeping camp had sprung to life. Uniforms were donned, faces washed, hair slicked back and cots made inside of fifteen minutes.

Then came the "monkey drill" and setting-up exercises, when the boys had to go through all sorts of grotesque but beneficial motions to exercise the muscles and stir the blood.

Of course there was some grumbling at first. Bart, who with all his physical fitness, liked to get his sleep out in the morning, had hard work to get his eyes open and feet on the floor at the same moment.

"Gee, how do you do it?" he grumblingly asked of Frank one morning, just after reveille and while he was rushing around with tousled head and one eye shut. "By the time I know I'm awake you're all ready, and worse than that, you look as if you enjoyed it. Gee, it's a gift!"

"You're like the man," Frank had remarked cheerfully, as he trussed up his trousers, "who was sentenced to die at daybreak. 'Oh, that's all right,' he answered. 'I never get up that early!' "

But the setting up exercises never failed to banish the last vestige of drowsiness, and by seven o'clock breakfast began to assume gigantic proportions. And how they ate!

After breakfast came the manual of arms, field practice, drilling in semaphore work and sometimes—this the boys looked forward to and enjoyed most,—a long hike in the spring sunshine to the exhilarating beat of martial music.

Then from eleven to two they did as they pleased and as dinner came within that period they mostly, to quote Billy Waldon, "wolfed."

The meals continued hearty and satisfying and as the days went on the boys broadened out and seemed, by the aid of muscular training and upright carriage, even to gain in height.

One morning Frank found a poem in a magazine he was reading and recited it to a group of laughing comrades. Thereafter it became the popular mess chant and the boys standing in line with their dishes would shout it out at the top of their lusty lungs to the great amusement of all concerned. It went something like this:

"You may mutter and swear at the reveille call
  With its 'Can't get 'em up in the morning;'
And you may not be fond of assembly at all
  But you drop into line at the warning;
Police call will cause you a lot of distress
  Though you answer at once or regret it,
But you jump when the splinter lips bugle for
    mess
  And the hash slinger yells, 'Come and get it!'"

Then came the chorus in which all joined:

"For you know that it means
  'Form in line for your beans
With your mess kit in hand—do it now!'
  And you cheerfully come for your coffee
    and slum,
  For your coffee and slum
When the splinter lips bugle for chow!"

It was all great fun, this jolly camp life, but
it had its serious side also. All the boys felt
the inspiration, almost exaltation of being one
of so great a body of men, men fired with the
same enthusiasm, the same great purpose to ac-
complish their glorious mission or die in the
attempt.

Training in the use of modern weapons of
warfare sobered the boys a little.

"I suppose I'm squeamish," said Bart to Frank one day, when they had finished a lesson in the throwing of hand grenades, "and I won't blame you or anybody else if you laugh at me. But I don't like those things. Every time I throw one I think of the possible mark it'll find some day in the German trenches and it makes me sick."

"Yes," said Frank, nodding gravely, "I know just how you feel, only it's the bayonet practice that gets me most. If those dummies were human instead of stuffed rags, I couldn't feel much worse about sticking the point into them."

"Oh, we're soft yet," said Billy, sauntering up to them. "I suppose it will take us quite some time to get hardened to this wholesale slaughter. But when we feel too squeamish, we want to remember the Belgian women and children murdered and tortured, defenseless old men slaughtered—"

"Yes," said Frank, his shoulders squaring and mouth setting grimly. "There's nothing like the memory of Dinant to make a fellow grip his bayonet!"

CHAPTER X

INSTRUMENTS OF DEATH

As TIME went on the boys became quite expert in bayonet practice. A French officer who had seen some of the bloodiest fighting on the Somme was their instructor, and he was voluble in his praise of the *"esprit de coeur"* the young men showed.

Of course in the beginning there were some laggards, but these were promptly whipped into line by officers and comrades.

"It is maybe all right now to laugh and take the little interest," the Frenchman was fond of saying to these few who lagged behind. "But when you are in the trench, fighting hand to hand with your enemy, more accomplished than you, it will not be so great a joke. You will not laugh then!"

"He's right too," remarked Fred Anderson, one of the veteran members of the regiment who had seen service in the Philippine Islands. There will be plenty of hand-to-hand fighting where it's cut and thrust, and the man who can handle his weapon best will come out on top."

"I suppose most of your own experience has been along that line," said Frank.

"Yes," replied Fred, as a reminiscent look came into his eyes. "Of course that dinky little war in the Philippines wasn't to be compared with this, but there was lots of savage fighting just the same. More than once I've been within an ace of losing the number of my mess."

"What's the tightest place you were ever in?" asked Bart.

"The thing I remember most was a scrap we had with the Moros," replied Fred. "That was pretty hot while it lasted.

"You see," he went on, "those fellows had been acting nasty and had given a good deal of trouble to one of our outposts. So our lieutenant was ordered to take a detachment in a launch and go up a little river that led to a settlement of theirs and give them a lesson.

"We landed at the nearest point and had about five miles of jungle to go through before we could get to their village. We did our best to make it a surprise, but in some way they got wind of our coming and lay in ambush. We were picking our way in single file when suddenly there came a rain of bullets and several of our men went down. The rest of us took to cover and the fight was on.

"The Moros you know are Mohammedans, and about as nifty fighters as you can find anywhere. Like all men of their religion, they believe that any one who dies on the battle-field goes straight to Paradise, and that gives them an absolute contempt for death. They were well armed too with Mauser rifles that they'd managed to get hold of somehow, but luckily for us they hadn't learned to handle them well and most of their shots went wild. If their shooting had been as good as their hearts were stout, they might have wiped us out, as they outnumbered us two or three to one.

"Has anybody got the makin's?" he inquired, as he stopped to roll a cigarette.

"Give them to him, somebody," said Bart exasperatedly.

"For the love of Mike don't keep him waiting!" ejaculated Frank. "I want to hear how Fred got out of it."

Fred, not a bit averse to the interest he had aroused, was tantalizingly slow in taking his time.

"Keep your hair on," he drawled, as he struck a match. "I got through all right, or I wouldn't be chinning to you now.

"Well," he resumed after a preliminary puff, "we kept picking them off whenever a head showed itself until they found that we could outplay them at that game, and then they resorted to other tactics. Throwing aside their guns and grasping their machettes—those murderous knives of theirs that will cut a man's head off with a single blow—they came charging down upon us. We didn't propose to stand on the defensive, and after a vast volley that swept a lot of them away we fixed bayonets and rushed to meet them."

The group that had by this time gathered about Fred drew a little closer.

"It was touch and go for a few minutes," continued Fred, "but our weight and discipline told, and soon we were pushing them back. Just then however I stumbled over a root and fell to the ground, striking my head and stunning myself. At that same moment the Moros were reinforced and came back with a wild rush that by sheer weight of numbers forced our line back for twenty-five feet or more.

"I was trying to get to my feet when four or five of the nearest Moros, brandishing their knives, swooped down upon me. It would have been all over with me, if one of our fellows, a big fighting Irishman named Hennessy, hadn't come plunging through the crowd swinging his rifle round his head like a flail. They went down like bullocks hit with an axe. They simply couldn't get inside the circle made by that gun and by the time he had knocked down a half dozen or more, our boys had rallied and had the beggars on the run."

"Phew, but that was a close shave!" ejaculated Frank.

"Close is right," agreed Fred. "I'd certainly have cashed in right then and there if it hadn't been for Hennessy. I told him that he had saved my life and that I owed him more than I could ever repay, but he wouldn't have it so. The joke of it was that I think he was really grateful to me for giving him a chance for such a lovely scrap. He told me that he hadn't enjoyed himself so much since the last time he had gone to the fair at Tipperary."

There was a general laugh.

"If it hadn't been for him, you wouldn't have had your chance now to get a hack at the Huns," remarked Bart.

"No," assented Fred, "and that would certainly have been hard luck. But to get back where we started from, I want to put it up to you fellows that what the Frenchman said was true. We can't take this practice too seriously. Especially bayonet practice. We've had lots of proof that the Germans don't like cold steel. They're brave enough, but the French and English put it all over them in bayonet work."

"That's right," agreed Frank, "and it's up to

us to show that Uncle Sam's boys can do the same."

The hand grenade throwing was of special interest to the boys and was the one most readily mastered. This was due chiefly to the fact that it had points in common with baseball. Many of the boys were proficient in the great national game.

The firm of Moore and Thomas had maintained its own nine, and in the season before they had carried off the championship of the commercial teams in Camport. Frank had officiated in the pitcher's box and had an assortment of curves and drops together with great speed that had been the chief factors in the winning of the pennant. Bart had "dug them out of the dirt" at first base.

Billy Waldon, too, had been as quick as lightning in "winging them down" from short.

So that their throwing arms were fully developed and they took up this new and grimmer game with the skill born of long practice.

"This ought to be nuts for us when we get to the trenches," remarked Billy, as he cut loose with a grenade in practice that landed within two feet of the object aimed at.

"It sure gives us a big advantage over the Germans," assented Frank. "Of course they're drilled in throwing, but by the time they've started in with it their muscles must seem strange to it. We've been throwing a ball around ever since we were kids. It's in the blood. Our eyes and arms have learned to work together. And then, too, a thing you've learned to do from the love of it must be better done than when it's forced on you."

"Imagine a crack pitcher with a grenade in his hand and the Kaiser a hundred feet away," said Billy with a grin.

"An A1 pitcher wouldn't do a thing to him!" chuckled one of the other recruits.

"Would he put over a bean ball or a fade-away, do you think?" asked Bart.

"It would be a strike-out, whichever one he used," declared Frank. "The Kaiser would do a fadeaway."

The bomb they used was the Mills bomb which had been adopted for general use in the British army.

"Let's hope there'll be plenty of them, whatever else we're short of," remarked Bart.

"They're handy little things to have around when the Boches come over for a friendly call," observed another lad.

"If we run short we can make some ourselves," declared Frank. "They won't be quite so nifty as these Mills bombs, but they'll do the work."

"Listen to Edison talking," chaffed Billy.

"I'm not kidding," declared Frank. "I got the tip from one of the Tommys who was wounded in the Ypres fighting and is over here on leave. Hustle around some of you chaps and get me an old tin can and I'll show you what the Tommy showed to me."

"What kind of a can?" asked Billy.

"Oh, any old kind," answered Frank." An old soup can, tomato can, any can that Eli hasn't eaten up already."

Eli was the big goat that served as the mascot of the regiment. He had an omnivorous appetite and ate anything from cigarette butts to washrags, and if anything was missing it was customary to charge it against Eli. He was not only a billygoat but a scapegoat.

A little search however brought to light an old can that Eli had spared, and the boys looked on with interest while Frank prepared his homemade bomb.

"I'll roll up my sleeves, gentlemen, to show you that I have nothing concealed there," said Frank, in his best conjurer's style. "Now watch me carefully and I'll try to instill some scientific knowledge in those thick noddles of yours."

He took a handful of clay from the edge of the trench where they had been practising and lined the inside of the can with it.

"Now for the dirty work," joked Billy.

Frank withered him with a glance.

"Get me a lot of junk," he commanded.

"That's rather indefinite," suggested Bart. "Junk shops are not a part of this regiment's equipment. Uncle Sam's had so much on his mind that he hasn't got to them yet."

"A handful of nails or bits of iron or cartridge shells will do," returned Frank, putting a detonator and explosive in the can and tamping it down in the clay. "Anything will do that will make Fritz see stars when it hits him."

Bart volunteered a broken jack knife; one lad contributed a couple of metal buttons; others handed over nails.

Frank arranged the miscellaneous collection in as compact a mass as possible, put in more clay and then put on the tin cover, into which he first punched a hole. Through this hole the top of the fuse protruded. Then he wrapped wire around the can so that the top could not come off, and the bomb was ready.

"There," he said, as he held his handiwork up for their inspection, "when that is sent over to the enemy trenches there will be something doing. It isn't much in the beauty line but it will get there just the same."

"Great head!" said Bart admiringly.

"Not mine but the fellow's who first figured

it out," said Frank. "But it's a good thing to know, and you never can tell when it may come in mighty handy."

"I hear we're going to be gassed to-morrow," remarked Bart, as they made their way to their quarters.

Billy made a wry face.

"That's one of the most hideous things the Huns have brought into this war," he said. "I can imagine Satan chuckling when he heard of the gas attack.

"I don't think he chuckled," said Frank bitterly. "More likely he was jealous to have a German think of it before he did. It isn't often that he lets anyone get ahead of him."

"He'll have to step lively to keep ahead of the Huns," said Bart. "They say there's no torture equal to that suffered by a man who has been gassed."

"And even if they don't die of it after days of agony, they might better have died," added another, "for it leaves them ruined for life."

"Surgeons get hardened in carrying on their profession," commented Frank. "They have to be or they couldn't keep their nerve. But they say that even the surgeons broke down when they stood beside the beds on which the gas victims lay gasping for breath. They had never seen such horrible anguish."

"Well, there's no use expecting Germans to carry on war like a civilized nation," declared Frank. "They've thrown all decency and humanity to the winds. They've raised the flag of the skull and crossbones and want to make all the rest of the world walk the plank. They're pirates and barbarians, and there'll be no peace or security for mankind until they're punished for their crimes."

"It's a tough job that's put up to us Allies," said Bart. "A man's job. But we'll put it through, no matter what the cost may be."

"Right you are," ejaculated Frank fervently. "It wasn't only Nathan Hale who wished that he had more than one life to give for his country. There are a million Nathan Hales among Uncle Sam's boys and millions more to come."

As Bart had predicted, their squad was lined up the next day for a practical test in gas defense. They had already had preliminary drills in adjusting the masks, which had to be slipped on in six seconds. It took a long time before this stage of excellence could be reached, for some of the men were doubly slow, slow in thought and slow in action. The quicker ones had soon acquired the habit of adjusting the masks in the required time, and Frank and Bart could do it sometimes in five seconds. But the drill went on unceasingly until all acted as one man, for a single second's delay in fending off the infernal attack might mean all the difference between life and death—and such a death!

It was not a pretty sight, for the masks were hideous and the men looked like weird monsters from another planet.

"If only our friends could see us now!" murmured Bart to Frank in an undertone.

"They'd drop dead from fright," returned the latter.

"Deep sea divers have nothing on us," chimed in a third lad.

"You're insulting the divers," said Billy. "If they went down looking like this, the sharks would throw a fit."

At last the drill worked with clock-work precision, and the perspiring lieutenant wiped his brow and gave vent to a sigh of relief as he looked along the grotesque ranks.

"I guess they're ready now," he said, turning to the sergeant. "Take them down half a dozen at a time and let them get a sniff of the gas."

"*Let* them." murmured a lad. "What a blessed privilege. Anyone would think that he was giving us a furlough for good conduct."

"Save your breath and come along," admonished Billy. "You'll need all you've got in a little while."

The squad was marched off to a little hut that stood in a distant corner of the camp. It was a crude creation with a door and only one window. Long before they got to it the boys could detect a faint acrid odor in the atmosphere.

"Now," said the sergeant halting his men at a little distance, "you fellows break ranks and come along in single file."

The single room of the hut had been filled with the same kind of gas that the Germans were using along the western front, but in greatly diluted form.

"Take off your masks," commanded the sergeant, "and go along past that window one by one. Make quick time too. I want you to learn just what the gas smells like, so that you can detect it the minute it comes near you after you get to the trenches."

The men obeyed orders, and, as they passed, each got a whiff of the gas that was escaping through a slight opening of the window. There was a gasp, a cough, a wry face and a hurried scuttling by as each man went through the ordeal.

It is needless to say that there was no disposition to linger. Even the slowest man of the squad displayed unsuspected capacity for speed.

"Look at Fatty Bates," chuckled Billy, alluding to the most ponderous member of the company. "Talk about winged heels! Mercury has nothing on him."

"It certainly got a rise out of Fatty," grinned Bart. "It's worth a dollar to see him jump. Put a gas cloud after him and I'll bet he'd do a hundred yards in ten seconds flat."

"You'll jump too when your turn comes," prophesied Frank. "You'll think the lid has been taken off of the infernal regions."

The prophecy was verified, for though there was no danger, since the gas had been vastly diluted, yet the odor was so vile and the death it suggested was so horrible that they could not get away from it quickly enough.

"It's like passing close to a rattlesnake whose fangs have been drawn," commented Frank. "You might know that he couldn't kill you, but if he struck at you you'd jump instinctively, just because he was a rattlesnake."

"Some perfume that," remarked Billy with an expression of dire disgust.

"New-mown hay—I don't think," growled Bart, sneezing as though he would shake his head loose from his shoulders. "I got a bigger dose than the rest of you slackers," he added with an air of superior virtue.

"Martyr to duty," mocked Frank. "But we're not through yet, fellows. The worst is yet to come."

"Nothing can be worse," grumbled Fatty Bates, with profound conviction.

"Oh, yes, it can," said Billy, assuming the role of Job's comforter. "We've got to go inside that Chamber of Horrors and stay there five minutes by the clock."

"Will we come out on our feet or be carried out?" asked Fatty Bates with a worried expression.

"You'll never be carried out, Fatty," chaffed Billy. "It would take the whole regiment to do that. It'll be a crane and derrick for you sure."

"We'll put a torpedo under him and blow him through the roof," added Bart.

"Now men," said the sergeant, "put on your masks and go inside, one after the other. There's no danger if you've learned to put them on perfectly. But if there's any sloppy work, the fellow that's careless will find it out soon enough, and he'll get all that's coming to him."

"Not much nourishment in that," muttered Billy under his breath. "Suppose the mask's defective, got a whole in it or something like that."

"If it is, it's better to find it out now than when we're actually in the trenches," answered

Frank. "I suppose that's the real reason for this test. Here's hoping that no shoddy contractor had put one over on the government."

They filed into the grim little room after having adjusted their masks with especial care and stood crowded closely together looking in their ghostly attire like so many spectres.

It was a grisly five minutes that seemed more like an hour to each one of them. The dead silence added to the discomfort of the occasion. Death seemed to be all around them, reaching out to them with its skeleton fingers. They were in the "valley of the shadow," and it sobered them.

It was an immense relief when the knock of the sergeant on the door summoned them forth and the test was over. And there was great satisfaction when it was learned that all the masks had held and shown that they could be relied on.

Once out in the clean, sweet air and under the blue sky that never before had seemed so beautiful, the boys tore off their masks in a hurry.

"Now I feel like a respectable member of society and not like one of the Ku Klux Klan!" exclaimed Bart, as he looked around on the flushed bronzed faces of his comrades. "My, but it's good to be out of this hideous rig. I'd like to throw it into the river," he added digging his fingers viciously into the unoffending mask.

"You'll be glad enough to have it some day before long," prophesied Frank. "Then you'll count it the best friend you have."

"Isn't it pretty nearly time for mess?" asked Fatty Bates wistfully.

"Not yet, little one," remarked Billy. "The sergeant's got something else up his sleeve, or I miss my guess."

A groan went up from Fatty, which was quickly suppressed when the sergeant looked sternly at him.

"Form in single file, men," commanded the sergeant, "and make your way through the trench. Bend over as you go, for you're supposed to be on the enemy front, and not a head must show to be a mark for snipers."

They did as they were told, and after they had reached a designated portion of the shallow trench they were halted by their leader.

"You're going to be gassed right and proper now," he said. "Some gas shells are going to be thrown over toward you and it's up to you when you see them coming to get those masks on mighty quick."

Crouching low and on the alert, the men waited until a gas shell with a hiss and a scream came hurtling in their direction and broke a hundred feet in front of the trench. A cloud of gas came rolling toward them. On went their masks in the twinkling of an eye, and the vapor passed over them harmlessly.

Several times this was repeated until the keen eye of the sergeant was satisfied with the dexterity shown by the squad. And there was a general sigh of relief when he summoned them out of the trench and announced that drill was over for the morning.

"Phew, but that was some strenuous work," remarked Frank, as holding their masks in their hands the men strolled back in groups of twos and threes toward their quarters.

"I feel as though I had been drawn through a knothole," said Fatty Bates.

The thought of Fatty being drawn through a knothole was so ludicrous that it provoked a general roar.

"I guess we all feel pretty well used up," said Bart when the merriment had subsided, "but all the same it's things like this that are going to help us lick the Huns."

And so the days passed in learning the grim lessons of war, and the shadows, lengthening into evening, brought supper, perhaps some special musical entertainment, a vaudeville show, or moving pictures, sometimes only bonfires with smoking, laughing, joking crowds about them. The boys enjoyed these latter evenings most when the funny events of the day could be passed in review and enjoyed by them all.

Then, promptly at nine the bugle called for "all lights out," and the young soldiers, early as was the hour, obeyed it willingly. The strenuous days in the open air made the narrow cots in the long barracks particularly appealing.

"Did you hear that joke Jameson was telling about the Yankee soldier?" Bart asked one night, when all the rest were either asleep or on the way.

"No," said Frank, sleepily. "What was it?"

"It seems a guard challenged him," chuckled Bart, "with the regular, 'Who goes there?' and he answered, 'Aw, you wouldn't know if I told you. I've only been here a couple o' days'."

"That's all very well here," yawned Frank. "But it wouldn't go in 'No Man's Land'!"

CHAPTER XI

NICK RABIG TURNS UP

"WHAT is that? Shrapnel?" asked Bart, one morning, as he opened his eyes after the reveille and heard the rain beating a tremendous tattoo on the roof.

"Hardly as bad as that," laughed Frank. "If it were, I bet you'd be out of that cot more quickly than you're doing it now. But it sure is coming down."

"So much the better," said Bart, as he jumped out and hastily began to dress. "That'll cut out the drill to-day and I'll have time to answer some of my letters and darn my socks."

But such roseate dreams were quickly dispelled. The storm increased in violence after breakfast and the wind blew great guns.

The Y. M. C. A. building was being erected for the use of that organization but was not yet completed. In the meantime, the Association had put up for temporary use a canvas tent, and as the storm increased in fury the flimsy structure gave every evidence of taking to itself wings and flying away.

The captain ordered a detail of men to go out and surround the tent and hold the tent pins down by main force if necessary.

There was nothing alluring about the prospect, for it meant a thorough drenching for the entire detail.

But the boys had already learned the first great rule of military life—to obey instantly any command given by a superior officer.

So Frank and Bart, who happened to be among those chosen for the work, jumped at the word. But they also had the soldiers' immemorial privilege of grumbling among themselves, and Bart chose to exercise it as they made their way in the teeth of the storm to the threatened tent.

"Just our luck to catch the captain's eye," he muttered.

"Stop your grumbling," adjured Frank. "Think how much worse it would be if we were plowing through the mud in No Man's Land. Let's make a lark of it."

"We'll be up among the larks all right," returned Bart, "if this thing ever gets away from the tent pins." They laid hold of the straining ropes and hung on for dear life. "An aviator would have nothing on us."

It was hard work while it lasted and their sturdy muscles were put to the test, but they had the satisfaction of keeping the tent in its place and after a while the storm subsided and the danger was over.

"Isn't it about time for those drafted men to get down here?" asked Frank, as they were on their way back to the barracks.

"I heard yesterday from Billy Waldon," returned Bart, "that two or three regiments were expected to-day. Up to now all the fellows here have been volunteers. I'm curious to see how the drafted men will take to the life."

"I suppose some of them will be sore at having had to come whether they wanted to or not," replied Frank. "Still there will be lots of good fighting material in them. I've heard Peterson say that the drafted men in the Union Army fought as well as the volunteers. They'll all be good Americans when they face the Huns."

Even as they spoke they heard the far-off music of a band and saw the men who were off duty hurrying toward the great gate of the camp.

"I shouldn't wonder if some of them were coming now," remarked Frank. "Let's leg it to the gate and see them come in."

They reached a favorable position just as the first of the advancing troops entered the camp. The boys studied them critically and in a somewhat patronizing spirit, for they already felt like veterans and were inclined to look down a little upon the "rookies."

There was, of course, a good deal to criticize about the newcomers. Most of them, up to a few days before, had never touched a gun in their lives, many of them were in civilian clothes, and although they tried to keep in line and step briskly to the music of the band, their marching was ragged.

Some of them, used to a sedentary life, were winded, even by that short hike of three miles to the camp. They were raw material in the fullest sense of the word. But the officers who led them and the men who watched them, knew perfectly well what wonders could be wrought in that outfit by a few weeks or months of training.

The regiment broke ranks as soon as they were fairly within the precincts of the camp.

"Look there!" cried Frank suddenly, as his eyes fell upon one of the near recruits. "If that isn't Tom Bradford, I'll eat my hat."

"Sure thing!" shouted Bart, as he looked in the direction Frank had indicated. "Hi there, Tom!" he yelled, and they both made a break for the place where Tom was standing.

In a moment they each had one of his hands and were shaking it as though they would wrench it off.

"Good old scout!" ejaculated Frank. "How in the name of all that's lucky did you get here?"

"Oh, I'm like a postage stamp?" grinned Tom, delightedly. "I stick until I get there."

"But I thought they wouldn't take you when you tried to enlist," said Frank, a little bewildered.

"Can you beat it?" returned Tom. "When I wanted to enlist they wouldn't have me. Then when I was moping along and raving against fate I was called up in the draft. The doctors there passed me without letting out a peep. Say, maybe I wasn't tickled to get in on any terms. It makes me sore though, to think I can't be in the old Thirty-seventh along with the rest of you fellows."

"Never mind," said Frank. "The main thing is, you're here. We'll be in the same camp and in the same division and we'll be able to see a lot of each other."

"I'm not the only Camport fellow that's here," chuckled Tom.

"Is that so?" said Frank with interest. "Who is it?"

"Give you three guesses," grinned Tom.

"Hal Chase!"

"Wrong," said Tom.

"Will Baxter!"

"Come again."

"Dick Ormsby!"

"You're all off," replied Tom. "But you'd never guess in a thousand years and so I'll put you out of your misery. It's Nick Rabig."

"Nick Rabig!" they yelled, in unison.

"Cross my heart and hope to die," laughed Tom, enjoying the amazement of his comrades.

"Nick Rabig, in a Yankee uniform!" chortled Frank.

"And going to fight the Huns!" crowed Bart. "Say, isn't it rich?"

"How does he feel about it," asked Frank, surprise and glee giving way to curiosity.

"Like a bear with a sore head," responded Tom. "Of course he doesn't dare to say much, but what he's thinking isn't fit for publication!"

CHAPTER XII

FOR FRANCE

THE young volunteers looked about for the unwilling conscript and soon caught sight of him, standing moodily apart from the others and with a scowl upon his face as black as a thundercloud.

"Papa's little sunshine," chuckled Frank.

"Same old cheery disposition," grinned Bart. "Say, if he looked at milk, he'd turn it sour."

"I suppose we ought to go over and speak to him," said Frank, thoughtfully. "He must feel like a cat in a strange garret."

"Maybe you're right," said Bart, doubtfully. "I'm willing to try anything once."

They strolled over to the place where Nick Rabig was standing and saluted him pleasantly.

"Hello, Rabig!" cried Frank. "How do you like your first look at our camp?"

"If it was the last look I'd like it better," snarled Rabig, his sullen resentment flaring forth at this unexpected sight of his old enemy.

"You'll change your mind, maybe, when you've had a chance to look around some," said

Bart, still trying to be agreeable, though the strain was telling on him.

"Yes," added Frank, "if there's anything we can do for you, let us know."

"The only thing you can do for me," said Rabig, his brows drawing together in a still blacker scowl, "is to get out of my sight and stay out."

"Oh, so that's all, is it?" said Frank with a careless laugh as they turned away. "Well, that's the easiest thing we ever had to do; eh, fellows?"

"You said it," they agreed as they walked on, leaving Rabig to glare after them with helpless hatred in his eyes.

After that, though they remained in camp several weeks, the boys saw little of Nick Rabig and were just as well satisfied. Friction was not in their line. They preferred the easy, happy comradeship that existed among nine-tenths of the fellows.

"I should think," said Bart, after a day of particularly hard but fruitful practice, "that we were almost ready to meet the Germans."

"Well, I don't know about that," returned Frank. "But I shouldn't wonder if we'd soon be sent over to France to finish our training behind the lines."

"Right you are," said Billy Waldon, strolling

up with Tom. "I overheard a couple of officers talking about the immediate plans for the regiment, and they seemed to think that we might expect orders almost any time to go to a camp nearer the sea."

"And from there I suppose we go across," said Tom.

"I hope that's right!" cried Frank, eagerly. "I'm just spoiling to get into action."

"All the fellows feel that way," said Bart.

"All but Rabig," put in Tom with a grin.

One day, the longed-for orders came and the camp with its thirty thousand men hummed with excitement and activity. About ten o'clock one bright sunshiny morning the regiment marched out of the gates of Camp Boone, to the martial music of its band, no longer a collection of raw recruits but a company of trained, vigorous young soldiers, ready and fit for any work their country might apportion them.

Two days and two nights they spent on the train and on the morning of the third day started the march to the camp which was to be their short abiding place.

"Say, fellows, you can smell the ocean!" cried Frank, drawing in deep breaths of the invigorating, salt-laden air. "Say, I'm not a bit anxious to get on it!"

"You'll be lucky," responded Bart, who was

hungry and therefore not as cheerful as was his wont, "if you don't find yourself under it before you get through. They say those submarines are doing pretty slick work."

"They may be doing now," said Frank whose high spirits refused to be dampened even by hunger, "but some day they're going to get done! You just let that sink home, Bart, my boy."

"I'd rather let some good juicy beefsteak sink home, just now," grumbled Bart, rebelliously. "If I have to feel like this much, I won't mind being sunk!"

An hour later, however, Bart's spirits had soared to ecstatic heights. His voracious appetite had been satisfied—and with beefsteak.

One night, less than a week later, a startling thing happened. The boys had turned in as usual sharp at nine o'clock, and were in the deep sleep of exhausted youth when they were suddenly awakened by the imperative notes of a bugle.

"Wh-what's that?" cried Frank, sitting up on his cot and straining his eyes through the darkness. "It's reveille—but it's dark as pitch."

"It c-can't be morning," stuttered Bart, while a babel of questions and answers arose all about them. "Gee, isn't six o'clock bad enough without getting routed out at—what time is it, Frank—my watch has gone on a strike."

"Just two o'clock," returned Frank, consulting his radio watch, while all about him was noise and confusion as the boys hastily got into their things. "I know what it is," he added, shouting to make himself heard above the din. "The time's come to sail and they didn't give us any warning for fear the news would get out! Bart, here's adventure for you!"

"Sure, I'll begin to enjoy it too," grumbled Bart, "when I get my eyes open."

The boys never forgot that ghostly march to the great transport which was to bear them across to the scene of conflict. No sound was heard, save the steady tramp, tramp of their feet, the occasional hoot of an owl far off in the woodland, and the eerie sighing of the wind among the trees.

When at last, after several miles of this weird marching, the huge, shadowy bulk of a ship rose before them, their hearts beat madly and they thrilled with a wild exultation.

Silently they marched on board. Then, the whispered commands of officers to men, the throbbing of the screws, the soft gliding of the great ship from the pier—and they were off!

"For France," murmured Frank, his eyes gleaming in the starlight. "For France and victory!"

CHAPTER XIII

THE LURKING PERIL

THE shipping of the men had been carried through so smoothly and swiftly, and everything had moved with such clockwork precision, that before the sun fairly rose the giant steamer was out of sight of land. And any spy who might have been lurking at any point on the coast would have had his trouble for his pains.

The night had been a broken one, but the army boys were so excited that no one cared for the loss of sleep. Here at last was action. Now they were fairly launched on the great adventure. Every mile that the great ship traversed was bringing them nearer to the scene of actual fighting, the roar of the cannon, the shriek of shells, the hand to hand conflict with the enemy.

"It must make the Huns sore," laughed Frank, "to think that one of their own great ships is carrying us over the ocean to fight the men who built it."

"Sort of poetic justice, eh?" grinned Billy Waldon.

"They felt they had the goods on us when they smashed the machinery," said Bart. "They figured it would take at least a year before we could get the ships in shape again, and yet its only five months since they scrapped the engines and here they're pounding along as good as new."

"It's not the first mistake the Kaiser's made," agreed Frank. "What was it that fellow Von Papen called us?—idiotic Yankees."

"We weren't so idiotic after all, that we didn't get on to his game and send him and his pals packing," said Tom.

"There goes the call for breakfast," cried Billy, as the bugle rang out its welcome summons. "This sea view is great but we'll have plenty of time to enjoy that. Me for the mess and we'll have to get in line quick or with this crowd we won't have a Chinaman's chance."

"Billy wants to eat while he can," grinned Bart, as they plunged along in his wake. "He's afraid he'll be seasick, later on."

"Not on your life," flung back Billy. "You can't get seasick on this ship. She's so big she rides half a dozen waves at once and she's as steady as a church."

Although the great ship was unchanged as regards the external appearance, a complete transformation had been effected inside. When it had first been built, it had been fitted out and decorated with princely magnificence but now all the costly and beautiful fittings had been ruthlessly torn out. It was like a great, hollow cavern from stern to stern. Everything had been sacrificed to the need for space. Cots and hammocks by the thousands took up every available inch that was not absolutely needed for other purposes.

It was a gigantic, floating hotel and apart from the crew, who themselves ran into the hundreds, it carried many thousands of Uncle Sam's fighting men.

"A U-boat would certainly make a ten-strike if it sent a torpedo into this craft," remarked Frank, as, after breakfast, the three friends secured a point of vantage on the upper deck.

"He'd get the iron cross from the Kaiser, sure enough," replied Billy. "It's so big a target that he could hardly miss it if he took a pot shot at it."

"I don't think there's much danger," said Frank, as he glanced at the guns with their trained crews that guarded the liner fore and aft. "If a U-boat attacked us she'd be the more likely of the two to get sunk. These guns outrange anything that a submarine carries."

"To say nothing of the convoys," put in Bart. "It's all right to attack an unarmed merchant ship but it's a different thing when United States destroyers are on the job."

"Where are they?" said Billy, looking about over the broad expanse which showed no trace of any other vessel.

"They'll meet us when we get further out," said Frank. "There will be no danger for a day or two yet. The U-boats are hugging the English coast pretty tight."

"I don't think we ought to reckon too much on that," said Billy. "You know, a U-boat did cross the ocean a year or so ago and sank five ships right off Nantucket. That's coming too close home for comfort."

"One swallow doesn't make a summer," replied Frank. "At that time we were neutral and after the U-boat once slipped past the British fleet there was nothing to stop it before it got to the American coast. But you bet it would be no cinch to do it now, with the United States navy on the job."

The next two days were fair and the sea smooth. The great liner reeled off the miles with tremendous speed. As Billy had prophesied, the ship was so steady that there was very little sea-sickness and there was so much to be seen and done under these novel conditions that every waking hour was filled with interest.

Two days later they picked up their convoy

and all felt a very comforting sense of security in the presence of the destroyers with their business-like air and wicked looking guns.

They kept pace with the liner, within easy reaching distance, occasionally exchanging signals, and keeping sleepless watch day and night over the huge transport.

"The finest navy in the world!" cried Frank, with enthusiasm, as his kindling eyes rested on these "bulldogs of the sea." "That's one branch of the service where Uncle Sam has never fallen down. Man for man, gun for gun, and ship for ship, there's nothing in the world can beat them. Just watch them clean out that U-boat nest when they once get over there in force."

"They'll do to them what Decatur did to the Barbary pirates years ago," said Bart. "Every other nation was paying tribute to them, but that idea didn't make a hit with us and we went in and wiped them off the face of the earth— or rather the face of the water. And what we did once, we can do again."

Frank's eyes had been idly roaming over the sea while they were talking, but suddenly his gaze became fixed and he started to his feet.

"Did you see that, fellows?" he demanded, sharply.

"Where?" asked Billy

"I didn't see anything," said Bart.

"It looked like a flash of light on the water," explained Frank. "There it is again. Great Scott, it's a periscope!"

Almost as he spoke, the forward guns on the liner roared their challenge, followed by the deeper bass of the guns from the nearest destroyer.

In an instant there was great excitement, though without the slightest trace of panic. The ship swung around in response to a bell from the bridge and began to zigzag in a bewildering fashion.

Then a great white furrow appeared in the sea and along that whitening lane came hissing a monster torpedo. Nearer and nearer it came with lightning speed straight toward the vessel.

Had the liner kept its course the torpedo would have struck it amidships. As it was, it passed just back of the stern, missing it by not more than a dozen feet.

The destroyers came racing like mad toward the spot from which the torpedo had been launched. No trace of the submarine was visible but the destroyers circled round and round the spot, dropping their deadly depth bombs in the hope of striking their unseen foe.

Thousands of pairs of eyes watched for the result, while in their excitement their owners almost forgot to breathe.

Minutes passed and then a mighty cheer went up. For on the waters appeared a gradually widening smudge of oil on which floated bits of wreckage that told their own story.

The U-boat had fired its last torpedo. One of the depth bombs had sought it out in its invisible lair, battered in its sides, wrenched open its seams and sent its pirate crew to their last account. For that one boat, at least, the Kaiser's admirals would watch in vain.

"We got it!" yelled Billy Waldon exultingly.

"They can't always get away with it!" cried Bart, jubilantly.

"What did I tell you about our navy?" crowed Frank. "They can't put one over on Uncle Sam!"

CHAPTER XIV

THE WAR-SWEPT LAND

"You've got to hand it to that fellow, though," said Billy. "He had his nerve right with him to try to cop out a transport right under the nose of a convoy."

"Yes," agreed Bart. "Although, after all, it may simply have been a chance meeting. The captain of the U-boat might have been as surprised as we were when he came up to breathe and found himself so close to us. But being there it was too good a chance to miss and he let fly."

"Maybe there wouldn't have been a high old time in Berlin if the torpedo had reached its mark," said Frank. "Think of being able to boast that they'd sunk thousands of Uncle Sam's troops! They'd have hung out the flags and rung the bells and given the school children a holiday."

"Well, a miss is as good as a mile," returned Billy. "It's a heap more comfortable sitting here and talking about it, than it would be to be in the water or rowing about in small boats while the submarine shelled us."

"Well, that particular submarine will never do any more shelling," said Bart. "It's all over with them now. It must be a fearful thing to die the way those fellows did, like rats in a trap. It's no wonder that the Kaiser finds it hard to get men to man his U-boats."

"It is pretty rough on them when luck goes against them," admitted Frank. "But if those fellows played the game fairly I'd feel sorrier than I do. Don't forget, that if they saw us struggling in the water they'd be standing on the deck of the submarine, if there were no destroyer about, grinning and mocking at us. And if women and children were drowning, it would make no difference to them."

"Right you are," declared Billy. "Do you remember what that U-boat did that sank the *Belgian Prince?* Smashed the small boats, threw away the oars, and took those of the crew who were left on top of the submarine."

"Yes," said Bart. "Then the Germans made everything tight and went below, leaving their prisoners on the deck. The U-boat sailed along the surface for a few hours and then slowly sank leaving their captives to drown. If that wasn't brutal, cold-blooded murder, there never was any in the history of the world."

"I hope this submarine was the one that did the trick," said Frank. "Perhaps drowning didn't seem such a rich joke to them when their turn came."

From that time on, the vigilance aboard ship was redoubled, for although the general opinion was that it was only a chance meeting, no one knew but what this U-boat was simply one of a fleet whose companions might look for better luck where their comrade had failed.

But nothing more was seen of the undersea terror until they were approaching the French coast and then the boys were witnesses of an exciting game that held them breathless.

"Look at that speck up there in the sky," exclaimed Frank.

"Biggest bird I ever saw," remarked Billy.

"That's no bird," declared Bart, after a prolonged inspection through a pair of glasses that he produced from his kit. "That's an aeroplane."

"An aeroplane!" exclaimed Billy. "So far away from shore as this? You're dreaming."

"You can see for yourselves," replied Bart, as he handed the glasses around. "Take a squint at it and you'll see that that bird never wore feathers."

"It must be a seaplane," announced Frank. "It's been launched from the deck of some vessel and now it's hovering up there like a hawk, looking for submarines. It's a funny thing, but they say that those seaplane pilots can look right down through the water and see a submarine when it can't be seen from the deck of a ship."

"What's the dope?" asked Billy, with great interest. "Suppose he does spot one, what good does it do?"

"He's got a wireless equipment," explained Frank, "and he sends out signals to trawlers and destroyers. They come on the jump and the seaplane tells them just where the submarine is lying."

"By jiminy, I think he sees one now!" exclaimed Tom Bradford, who had just come up. "See that smudge of smoke over there? That means a steamer's coming and there's another."

As though by magic one boat after another hove in sight until there were four, coming from as many points in the compass and heading toward that point in the sea over which the seaplane hovered.

The boys were on edge with excitement at the prospect of being in at the death and as the liner was rapidly approaching the scene of action, they had a clear view of what followed.

Guided evidently by signals from the seaplane, two of the trawlers stretched a long chain between them and advanced slowly toward the other two who, with a similar chain approached from the other direction.

"What do you suppose they're trying to do?" asked Billy, curiously.

"The idea is, to get those chains under the submarine," explained Frank. "After they've done that, they'll crisscross them from above. If they once succeed in doing it the sub is done for. He's got to come up and surrender or else they'll slip him a depth bomb and blow him to flinders."

Deftly and quickly the work went on under the direction of the skilled veterans who held command of the trawlers. Then they waited for the submarine to come up.

But it did not come. Instead, it released a group of mines on the chance of wrecking one or more of its captors. But they were on the lookout for just such a contingency and fended off these "floating deaths," waiting till they had finished their more important work before rendering them harmless.

Minutes passed and still the U-boat lay like a sullen monster, trapped but not subdued.

Then it was the trawlers' turn to take the offensive. Two depth bombs were placed on the taut chains and slid down through the waters to the hull of the doomed submarine.

There was a muffled boom, a geyser-like rush of water, and then the telltale oil that came to the surface showed that all was over. One more of the assassins of the sea had paid the score it owed to an outraged world!

"And that's the Kaiser's weapon that was going to bring England to her knees!" ejaculated Tom.

"The Allies are getting the best of them," declared Frank. "It looked at one time as though Germany were going to put it over. But we're sinking them now just as fast as they can be built and when America gets fairly to work we'll sink them still faster."

"Just wait till Edison gets on the job. He'll find something that will finish the U-boats in jig time. He'll make them look like thirty cents," declared Tom.

A little later they caught their first sight of France. Only a blur on the horizon at first, it grew steadily larger, and the bow of the boat was packed with the eager young soldiers, straining for a sight of the war-swept land that had suffered so much and done so much in the fight for liberty and democracy.

Here they were to fight, here they were to suffer, here they were to carry their country's flag to a glorious victory!

Frank breathed hard as the land came closer, for to him France had a greater significance than even to the others. It was his mother's land and for that reason doubly dear.

As the great vessel followed by others drew
near the port, it was seen that the wharves and
shores were black with people. News had been
wirelessed of their coming, and the city had
gone wild with joy at this visible token of help
from the great sister republic across the sea.

Bells were ringing, whistles blowing, cannon
booming. Flags were flung out from all the
buildings and the whole city was in holiday
garb to welcome Uncle Sam's army boys to
France!

CHAPTER XV

WITHIN THE SOUND OF GUNS

"HERE at last!" cried Frank in wild jubilation, as the transport was made fast to the wharf. "Pinch me, fellows, to make sure I'm not dreaming."

"It's real, sure enough!" exulted Bart.

"Now we'll see action!" exclaimed Billy.

"And get a chance at Fritz and Heinie!" added Tom. "I'm aching to get a hack at them."

Frank did not answer to this. Now they had arrived in France his mind had drifted back to his mother and what she had said about the property she had inherited. Would they ever be able to claim his grandfather's estate?

If the army boys could have had their way, they would have leaped forthwith from the deck to the dock. They were wild to feel the soil of the gallant country beneath their feet. But discipline had to be observed and several hours elapsed before the troops were ready to leave the ship.

Then at last they poured over the gangplank, line after line, wave after wave, in what seemed to the delighted multitude of watchers an almost endless procession.

They formed in line and after a formal exchange of greetings between their commanders and the city authorities, the troops swung into the streets with the bands playing alternately, the "Star Spangled Banner" and the "Marseillaise."

Such cheers as greeted them, such tears, such pelting of flowers, such waving of flags as the stalwart young Americans marched through streets that were packed to the curb with joyous, shouting, frenzied natives!

It was a royal greeting that not one of the boys could ever forget.

They reached the great barracks that had been assigned to them by the French Government for a temporary halting place before they should go to a place in the interior right behind the fighting lines.

There was plenty of room, for the barracks were empty now, every son of France of fighting age that could be spared, being at the front.

"They sure seemed glad to see us," grinned Frank, as, after the march, the regiment broke ranks and the men went to their quarters.

"I don't wonder," replied Bart. "I suppose America felt the same way a hundred years ago when Lafayette and his comrades went over there."

"Gee, it seems strange to speak of America as being over there," said Tom, a little soberly.

"Not getting homesick, are you, Tom?" questioned Billy, with a smile.

"I have an idea I will," Tom answered with a grin, "when I have time to think about it. But it would make me sicker still," he added stoutly, "to go back before we'd licked the Huns."

"Right-o!" cried Billy. "When I go back I want to take a lot of German helmets along to give to some girls I know."

"*Some* girls," chaffed Bart. "You talk like a Mormon, Billy."

The next few days were busy and delightful ones for the boys. The townspeople opened their hearts and homes to them, and they were feasted and entertained to their heart's content. Everything was so new and strange to them that they were constantly stumbling upon surprises.

The language, to be sure, offered some obstacles. The boys had been taught some of the most necessary French phrases while in their training camp, and these along with some language primers they carried, sufficed for their more simple needs. But their vocabulary was limited and their accent was a fearful and wonderful thing, though their hosts were too polite to laugh at them.

Frank had some advantage over the others because his mother, being a French woman, had taught him her native tongue, and it was a great comfort to the rest of the Camport boys to have Frank along with them as interpreter when they themselves were stumped—which, it must be confessed, was often!

Tom especially, who had no gift for languages was usually in hot water. His struggles with the language were frantic, not to say pathetic.

"You're game, old scout," chaffed Billy, after Tom had wrestled in vain with the pronunciation of the French word for soup. "But why in thunder did you make that waiter crazy by asking for bullion? Any one would think you were trying to cop off the United States mint."

"Well, what should I say?" Tom defended himself stoutly, as he thumbed over his phrase book. "There it is, plain as day," he added, triumphantly—"b-o-u-i-l-l-o-n. If that isn't bullion, what is it?"

"You're all wrong, you're all wrong," said Bart condescendingly. "It's *bwe-yone,* just like that."

Tom tried it once or twice desperately and then gave it up.

"I'd have to have a cold in my head to talk that way," he protested, pocketing the book in disgust. "I'm not going to try any more. The more I try the worse I get. The next time, I'm going to ask for soup, plain, old fashioned American soup. S-o-u-p. Get that? Then the waiter can do the guessing!"

"Yes, and then he'll serve you spaghetti," laughed Frank.

"So much the better," grinned Tom. "Let him go through the whole shooting match. Sooner or later he'll come to soup and when he does I'll be there."

"And you intend to eat right through the menu?" queried Billy admiringly.

"The which?" asked Tom. "Oh, you mean the bill of fare. Sure thing. I don't care whether it's soup to nuts or nuts to soup, I'll catch it coming and going."

"And you're the fellow they wouldn't let enlist on account of his teeth," moaned Billy, with a doleful shake of his head.

"They didn't know me," grinned Tom.

The army boys spent nearly a week in the barracks to get rid of their "sea legs," and then the order came to go to the new camp, right behind the lines that had been assigned to them.

It was too far for a hike and the railroads

were taxed to their capacity in taking supplies to the forces at the front. But the problem was solved by a multitude of gigantic motor trucks, *lorries,* in which two score of men could find accommodation.

They were high-powered machines capable of tremendous speed and they rushed over the fine French highways like so many express trains.

"This is the thing that saved Paris," remarked Frank. "If Gallieni hadn't packed all his troops and rushed them up as reinforcements, France would have lost the battle of the Marne."

"They're great goers all right," commented Bart. "We're sure breaking the speed laws. But I don't see any traffic cops stopping us."

"They'd only cheer us on," grinned Tom. "We can't get to the battle lines too quick to suit the French."

Up hill and down dale they raced, through thriving cities, and quaint villages, past peasant cottages and princely chateaux, lying beautiful and serene in the bright sunshine.

They were in the garden spot of France, a place that had yet been spared the horror and devastation of war, and the only thing that seemed unnatural was the striking absence of young men.

Women everywhere were doing the work, in the fields, in the stores, at the railroad stations, on the streets and country roads. Scarcely any males were seen except old men and boys.

There was no need to ask where the young men were. At Verdun, on the Somme, on the Aisne; everywhere on that long line of trenches that stretched from the Vosges to the sea, they were fighting like heroes to keep the Hun at bay.

And on the heart of each were written those immortal words spoken at Verdun: *"They shall not pass!"*

Hour after hour went by. Suddenly Frank asked:

"What was that, fellows? Did you hear it?"

"Sounded to me like thunder," said Bart.

"With a sky like this?" replied Frank. "Never. Listen!"

Borne on the wind came a long, booming sound, growing longer and louder as they sped toward it, falling fitfully at times, only to swell into a mightier rumble like the roar of waves dashing against the coast.

They looked at each other with comprehension dawning in their eyes.

"It's thunder all right, Bart," said Frank, quietly. "It's the thunder of the guns! We are getting near the fighting front at last!"

CHAPTER XVI

THE AIRSHIP RAID

THE signs multiplied now that they were approaching the battle lines. Apart from the ominous roar which had now become unceasing, war showed its grim face on every hand.

They dashed through "rest billets"—the towns behind the lines where the exhausted soldiers, who had served their term in the trenches, were sent back for a few days or weeks of rest while fresh troops took their places.

The roads became more congested with trucks carrying supplies and ammunition to the front. Ambulances came past in an endless stream, bearing their quota of wounded men. Hospitals were everywhere, marked with a Red Cross that bespoke their mission of mercy and healing.

And there were cemeteries too, with their endless rows of simple wooden crosses on which were inscribed the names and regimental numbers of those who slept beneath.

Cripples, too, there were, with missing legs or arms, and blinded ones, who had looked for the last time on scenes of warfare.

It was the seamy side of war that thrust itself upon their sight. But though it sobered, it
did not daunt these eager young Americans who
had come to do their part and "see it through."
It only deepened their indignation at the merci-
less military power that had brought such woe
and misery upon the world, and each breathed
a vow to himself that he would not rest until
that power was curbed and punished as it deserved to be.

"This looks like the real thing," remarked
Frank.

"That's what!" agreed Bart. "You can see
already that war is what Sherman said it was."

"This is nothing," put in Billy. "It's only
the fringe. It's only when we get in the
trenches that we'll know anything about it."

"Some of us may not know much then," put
in Tom. "It all depends on how long we succeed in dodging the bullets."

"Yes," observed Billy. "Or our experience
may be like that of the Tommy who said 'First,
I 'ears a 'orrible noise and the next thing I
'ears the nurse sayin', "Sit up and drink this!'"

There was a laugh that broke the tension, and
before long they reached the district that had
been chosen for their intensive training.

It was a wide stretch of rolling country several miles in extent, and it had been chosen

because it resembled in its main features the actual territory where the fight was going on.

There were brooks and hills, valleys and quarries, woods and meadowlands with a few small hamlets of scattered houses.

There were no spacious barracks such as they had been used to in the cantonments at home. The troops were quartered here and there as opportunity offered.

Thousands of dog tents had been erected on the level places and in these the majority of the men were sheltered.

Every cottage and chateau also had its quota, and farmhouses with their outlying barns and stables were utilized to the utmost.

"Hope they don't separate us, fellows," said Frank, as he watched the corporals and sergeants picking out various squads and assigning them their billets.

"Gee, so do I," echoed Bart. "The old bunch has been together ever since we left Camport and I have a hunch our luck's going to continue."

The "hunch" proved to have a solid foundation, for the four army boys were all sent off together with about forty more of their comrades to an old mill that stood near the edge of the camp.

It was a low, rambling structure with plenty

of windows that gave it ample light and an air of homely comfort that delighted the young soldiers.

"This is what I call luck," chortled Tom, as he looked about him and glanced up at the well-thatched roof that seemed rain-proof.

"It beats a dog tent by a thousand miles," returned Billy.

"It doesn't matter so much while the weather's still warm," said Bart, "but oh, boy! when the winter comes, maybe it won't be good to have a snug roof like this over our heads."

A little cottage adjoining the mill served as a mess hall for the squad billeted there and the presiding genius of the place was a French cook, who had as his assistant a young Irish lad whose most prominent points were a shock of red hair and a mischievous disposition.

"Anatole is a good chef, all right," Frank remarked one day, shortly after they had had a most appetizing meal. "He may have his faults and probably does, but he cooks to beat the band."

"Yes," agreed Bart, "he's a dandy cook but he's got a hair-trigger temper. I've heard him bawling out his helper in all the French epithets there are, and that's quite a few apparently."

"Righto!" laughed Frank. "There's a big lot of them and Anatole knows them all. He could give points to the driver of a team of army mules. You've got to hand it to him for being thorough anyway. Without that outlet he'd probably go crazy."

"Possibly," assented Bart. "There's no telling. But listen. 'Speak of the cook and you'll hear him shouting' or words to that effect. Great Scott! He's mad for fair this time."

"You've said it!" ejaculated Frank. "He's about as angry as it's possible for a Frenchman to be—and that's going some."

Fate had willed that that day the Irish helper in a spirit of impish perversity should have annoyed the cook in various covert and ingenious ways until the latter's irritation broke all bounds.

The cottage door flew open and the boy bounced out, about two jumps ahead of the cook whose face was crimson and eyes bulging.

"Pat has an air of haste about him," remarked Frank with a grin.

"He'd better have," laughed Bart. "Anatole is up in the air for fair."

"Leetle rat zat you air!" shouted the enraged cook, shaking a ladle furiously at his helper who stood at a safe distance wearing a tantalizing grin. "Sacre! but you drive me cr-r-r-azy weet your seely tricks. You air one Irish monkey, zat ees what you air! Ef I get hol' of you—ah, you weel not forget eet soon, I tell you zat!" and he made a clumsy rush for the boy who easily dodged around a corner of the cottage. The cook raced after him and the pair made several circuits of the little building, although it was evident that the cook had absolutely no chance of catching his agile tormentor.

They made a highly ludicrous sight, and Frank and Bart, who happened to be the only spectators of the scene, roared with laughter, stamping about and hammering each other on the shoulder in the excess of their merriment. But the cook was not long in discovering the futility of his efforts and gave up the chase, puffing and blowing like a grampus. His wrath had in nowise abated however, and he shook his fist impotently at the boy, who by his very silence and the ease with which he eluded him drove the unfortunate chef into a very paroxysm of fury.

"*Mille tonnerres!*" he shouted, and hurled the heavy ladle he had been carrying straight at his assistant's head. But the lad ducked in time, and the heavy missile went whistling past him and found lodgment in the underbrush beyond.

"Better luck nixt toime," jeered the imp. "Try agin, why don't ye? Ye've got plinty uv thim ladles left. 'Tis the bist uv exercise, throwin' thim things is."

Frank and Bart shouted afresh, while the outraged cook tore his hair in desperation and gave vent to a stream of epithets. The boy said nothing, but put his hand to his ear and affected to listen in a manner far more irritating than words could possibly have been.

The cook's face grew more crimson than before and his naturally protruding eyes seemed about to leave their sockets. He danced wildly about, shaking his clenched fists madly in the air. At last however, just when he seemed threatened with a stroke of apoplexy, he stopped from sheer exhaustion and for the first time became conscious of the presence of Frank and Bart who were leaning on each other for support, convulsed with laughter and the tears streaming from their eyes.

He glared malevolently at them for a few moments but finding that this had little effect at last turned and went into the cottage still muttering imprecations on the head of his assistant.

"Help, help!" gasped Frank. "Hold me up, Bart, or I'll go down. My, but that was rich."

"All of that," agreed Bart, wiping the tears from his eyes. "If we'd only had a moving picture machine and a phonograph handy to take down that scene. It would be the biggest hit of the age."

"It would have meant oodles of coin and no mistake," assented Bart. "We'd have been beyond the reach of want for the rest of our natural lives."

"Anatole's got a circus clown beaten by a thousand miles," replied Frank. "It's too bad that the rest of the fellows couldn't have been here to see the circus. But I suppose it's ungrateful to criticize fate after she's been so kind to us."

"I should say so," chuckled Bart. "If I live to be a hundred years old, I never expect to see anything funnier," and at the remembrance of the comical scene he started laughing afresh with his hand pressed against his side.

"Just the same," said Frank, when they had at last quieted down, "I wouldn't like to be in that red-headed helper's shoes. He's got to go into the cottage soon, and when he does I have a hunch that something will happen to him."

"I think it's extremely likely," agreed Bart, "and I can't say but what he deserves it. It seems to me that Anatole has something coming to him in the way of revenge."

It was with considerable amusement that the two chums watched the actions of the Irish lad. For some time he kept clear of the cottage, but then the door opened and the cook's head appeared in the doorway.

"Come here, you Mickey!" he called, in tones meant to be reassuring, "and peel ze potatoes."

With a good deal of caution the boy reluctantly approached, but stopped just out of the cook's reach for a parley.

"Wot ye goin' ter do wit' me whin ye git holt uv me?" he queried. "I wuz only foolin' wit' ye before. Can't ye take a little joke?"

"Nevaire mind," replied the cook realizing his advantage. "Come an' get beezy, else I tell ze captain you air—wat you call eet?—inzubordinate. Zen he make you come."

The boy glanced desperately around in search of some way of escape from his predicament, but finding none finally went reluctantly into the cottage.

"Here's where retribution falls on him," said Frank with a grin.

He was not mistaken, for the boy had scarcely entered when there issued forth the sound of several lusty smacks. Then came a high-pitched scolding which showed that Anatole had had recourse to moral as well as physical suasion.

"I don't know but what I'd rather have the licking than the scolding," chuckled Bart as they listened to the voluble eloquence of the chef.

"Either one's bad enough," laughed Frank. "I guess our young red-headed friend has got all that was coming to him."

Now the intensive training of the boys began in earnest. And training now had a meaning that it had never had while they were still on American soil.

For at that time they had not fully grasped the fact that they were actually at war. There had been a certain dream-like quality about it that had been like a scene from a play.

The only cannon they had heard were those fired in salute or at practice. The zip of a bullet had only meant that that bullet was speeding toward a wooden target.

But now the roar of cannon, multiplied a thousand fold above everything they had heard before, meant that deadly missiles were seeking out human life in an effort to maim and destroy.

And soon—how soon they did not know, but still soon—they themselves would be the target for whining bullets and shrieking shells.

Practice now meant something. Expertness might mean the difference between saving life or losing it. A new spirit ran through the men like an electric current. No need now for their officers to urge them on. If anything, they had to hold the young soldiers back, lest they burn up their vitality and exhaust their strength before they were put to the final test.

As far as possible, the camp became a mimic battlefield. Trenches were dug, precisely like those that they would soon be holding against the attacks of the enemy.

Barbed wire fences were built by one regiment and cut through and beaten down by another, which, for the time being, was chosen to play the part of the enemy.

The bayonet practice was no longer against dummies but against a picked squad of their own comrades. And each side in these mimic battles was so eager to win that at times they almost forgot themselves, with slight wounds and bruises as a result before their officers could intervene.

"We're getting there, Bart!" cried Frank, as he wiped the perspiration from his brow, after a particularly strenuous encounter. "I'd back our boys right now to hold their own against any bunch of equal size that the Boches can send against them."

"We sure are doing dandy work," assented Bart. "I wonder when they're going to put us on the firing line?"

"Before long I hope," chimed in Tom. "I'm aching to get a whack at them. It's the only way I can let off steam," he added, ruefully. "I came near running one of the boys through with my bayonet to-day."

"I wonder where they'll put us," conjectured Billy. "I suppose they'll sandwich us in with some of the French troops for a while until we get our bearings."

"Maybe," said Frank. "But I'd like better to have us fellows take up some sector and hold it all by ourselves. The tri-color's a fine flag, but when I fire my first bullet at a Hun I want to be under the Stars and Stripes."

"You've said it!" declared Tom.

"You fellows are regular fire-eaters," laughed Dick Lever, a young fellow with whom the boys had struck up a friendship.

He wore an aviator's uniform and was a fine type of young American. He was one of those who, on seeing war impending, had not waited for the formal declaration, but, at their own expense, had sailed to the old country to help France and, so doing, the United States.

Bronzed, upstanding, clear-eyed, he had succeeded in making the army boys like him immensely and had imparted to them many useful and interesting stories of modern warfare.

"You're a good one to talk," said Billy. "When it comes to fire eating, you aren't so slow yourself. I heard from one of the fellows yesterday what you did at the battle of the Somme."

Dick blushed like a girl.

"That was nothing," he protested. "Just part of the day's work."

"What's the dope?" asked Tom with interest. "I haven't heard the story, and from the beginning, it ought to be good."

"Will Scott was telling me about it," said Billy. "He says that Dick here went over the German lines and started a little war all by himself. He flew low near the ground, letting loose his machine gun at a whole regiment of German soldiers just forming up for action. Went along a little further and lambasted a bunch of German officers in an automobile, killed two of them and made the others jump out and hide under the machine. Then came back and, just for good measure, let fly his machine gun at the same regiment he'd soaked going out. After that I guess he knocked off and called it a day's work.

"That's why he wears that decoration," he added, pointing to the cross on Dick's jacket.

"See him blush," chaffed Tom. "It's funny how these fellows that can face any number of bullets, turn coward when it comes to praise. You'd almost think we were accusing him of a crime."

"Any other of the boys would have done the same if he had had my chance,'" said Dick. "Sometimes I go days at a time without having a chance for a scrap. That just happened to be my lucky day."

"The Huns didn't call it that," laughed Frank.

Dick who, as a matter of custom, had been scanning the sky, uttered a sharp exclamation.

"Here's another bit of luck, fellows, perhaps," he cried, and without further farewell, was off like a shot toward his machine, which had been waiting, with his mechanic to guard it, a hundred yards away.

High up in the sky appeared a squadron of airships that by their markings and designs the boys recognized as enemy planes. They were evidently bent on adventure and had come much further beyond the lines than usual.

The French were quick to accept the challenge and the anti-aircraft guns got into action at once. Puffs of shrapnel burst like white clouds in and about the marauding planes.

Even as the boys watched, one missile found its mark, and the plane, out of control, whirled round and round and then fell swiftly to the ground within the French lines.

But not with guns alone did the Allies respond. Like a flock of falcons, a squadron of

French aeroplanes shot swiftly up into the air, climbing, climbing in the effort for altitude, so that they might swoop down upon their prey from above.

"There goes Dick's plane in the van!" cried Frank, his voice tense with excitement.

"That's the place for America!" exclaimed Tom. "Always in the van!"

CHAPTER XVII

THE BAPTISM OF FIRE

ALL faces were turned toward the sky. It was the army boys' first glimpse of a battle in the air and the grim game held them spellbound.

Like great birds the battle planes wheeled and swooped, now diving, now climbing, each jockeying so as to get the weather gauge of its opponent and bring its machine guns into action.

The forces were nearly equal and for some time victory hovered in the balance. But either the staying quality or the alertness of the Allies finally turned the scale. Two of the enemy planes were shot down, and a third, evidently crippled, but not wholly out of control, sought the ground within its own lines.

The German force, now depleted, turned east and made off at full speed, with the Allies in hot pursuit.

Then the sky clouded over and the finish of the fight was lost to the eager watchers below. But they had seen enough to know that the raiders had been beaten back and that victory rested with the Allies and they were jubilant at the result.

"The Huns went back quicker than they came," gloated Tom.

"Right-o!" cried Bart, gleefully. "They came to shear and they went back shorn."

"The Kaiser, he has lost his sheep
    And doesn't know where to find them,
Leave them alone and they'll come home
    With our planes close behind them."

So parodied Billy.

"I hope Dick comes out of it all right," said Frank, a little soberly.

"Trust that boy," said Tom, confidently. "I don't imagine anyone needs to worry about him. If he can't take care of himself, nobody can."

But the Germans, though beaten in that skirmish, were far from being discouraged, and the boys were to learn that very night with what a persistent foe they had to deal.

It had been a hard and exciting day and now, after a steaming hot supper, they were scattered about the old mill in comfort and utter relaxation.

Some were smoking, others chatting, some mending their clothes, which in these days of strenuous work were often in need of repair, while one or two by the light of candles were writing letters to the folks at home.

Billy, seated on a stool, was strumming a banjo which had been his solace many a time while he was stationed on the Mexican border and which now was doing duty in France.

"Hit 'er up, Billy," said Bart, lazily. "We don't mind being miserable if it gives you any comfort."

"Quit your knocking," grinned Billy. "You know you're just dying to hear it. What do you fellows want—the Moonlight Sonata or something else simple like that?"

"That's too high class for this bunch," said Tom. "Though there's plenty of moonlight outside," he added, as he looked out the window.

"I've had all the outside I want for one day," said Frank. "I'd just as soon stay where I am." He was penning a letter to his mother, telling her of many things that had happened, and stating that, so far, he had not had a chance to learn anything about his grandfather's estate.

"Well, I'm waiting," said Billy. "What does the gang want? Jazz band music? That's about your style."

"No, give us something that sounds like home," said Tom. "Some of those southern melodies."

"Yes," urged Bart. "You're a dabster at that, Billy."

"All right," said Billy, cheerfully. "Anything to oblige."

He picked the strings for a moment and then began to sing softly—

> "Swing low, sweet chariot
>   Gwine for to ca'y me home
> Swing low, sweet chario—ot
>   Gwine for to ca'y me home."

Bang! There was a tremendous explosion close to the mill. The air was filled with a deafening din.

The boys jumped to their feet.

"That hit mighty close!" cried Frank.

"What do you suppose it was?" came from Tom. "A shell?"

"We're too far away from the German lines for that," replied Bart.

"More likely it's a bomb from an airship," said Frank. "Let's take a squint outside and see."

They rushed out and their first glance was toward the sky. But there was nothing visible there, nor could they hear the whirring of motors that was the invariable accompaniment of air raids.

But when they searched around the mill they were more successful, for the bright moonlight revealed a freshly dug hole in the ground that formed a veritable crater.

"It was a bomb all right," pronounced Frank. "And from the size of the hole it made it was a lallapalooza. It's lucky it didn't hit the mill."

"I guess some Hun aviator was flying back to his own lines and dropped this as a sort of visiting card," said Billy. "Oh, well, what's a little bit of bomb between friends? Come on back, fellows."

"Yes, come along in and listen to Caruso," chaffed Tom.

Once inside, Billy again picked up his banjo and began to croon.

> "It rained all night the day I left
>   The next day it was dry.
> The sun so hot I froze to def
>   Suzanna, don't you cry."

One after another took up the rollicking chorus—

> "Oh, Suzanna,
>   Don't you cry for me,
> "Fur I'se gwine to Alabama
>   Wif de banjo on my knee."

Bang! Bang! Bang! came three quick explosions, blending in a tremendous roar.

At the same instant a hole appeared in the roof. Part of it caved in and came clattering down while a blinding glare filled the room!

CHAPTER XVIII

A GRIM REALITY

THE strumming ceased and the banjo fell to the floor. For a moment confusion reigned supreme.

The shock and the glare had a paralyzing effect but it lasted only for an instant. Then the army boys pulled themselves together.

"Is anyone hurt?" shouted Frank, as he looked about him.

A groan came from a distant corner. They rushed in that direction.

Fred Anderson was trying to struggle to his feet and in an instant willing arms supported him. His face was pale, blood was flowing from a gash in his forehead and his right leg crumpled up beneath him as he tried to bear his weight upon it.

"I guess the old pin's gone back on me, boys," he said with a faint attempt to smile. "I don't seem to have any feeling in it. I guess the Huns got me that time."

A quick examination showed that the leg was broken just below the knee.

They quickly improvised a temporary splint and a field ambulance was called. The gash in the head proved to be only a flesh wound of no great importance. But it bled freely and gave the impression that Fred was dangerously, perhaps mortally wounded.

It was the first time that these young novices in the art of war had seen blood flowing from American veins from a wound inflicted by a German, and it brought home to them that they were really in the war and might at any instant, like their luckless comrade, come to hand grips with death.

"That sure was a close call," remarked Frank, after Fred, having been made as comfortable as possible, had been carried off by the ambulance to the field hospital. "It might have blown us all to bits."

"That roof may be all right to keep out rain," said Billy, "but it wasn't built for bombs."

"It must have been a glancing blow," commented Tom. "If it had come plump through our name would have been Dennis. It must have spent most of its force on the ridge pole and slid off to the ground."

"Very considerate of it," said Bart, dryly.

"There may be more where that came from," suggested Billy. "There may be a whole squadron of Hun flyers up there in the sky."

"I guess it will be healthier to stay outside for a while," said Tom. "We can see the bombs coming and dodge them. It will be a new kind of outdoor sport."

"It's a new game all right," Bart flung over his shoulder as they made their way outside. "And a game where the stakes are high. You pay dearly if you lose."

They all reached the open, where they found that the entire camp had been aroused by the nocturnal raid. They quickly learned from their excited comrades that other billets had been targets for the marauders and that several soldiers had been severly injured, while one was killed.

Searchlights were sweeping the sky in the attempt to locate the hostile planes. Anti-aircraft guns were popping, and the French escadrille had already mounted to give battle.

"There comes one!" shouted Frank, as his keen eyes caught sight of a tiny blaze coming through the air. "That's the fuse of a bomb."

"And it's coming right toward us!" yelled Bart. "Run fellows—quick!"

They needed no second injunction and it was well they moved quickly, for a moment later, the messenger of death came down close to the spot where they had been standing and exploded with a tremendous roar.

But they had thrown themselves flat on their faces, behind whatever shelter they could find and the rain of iron missiles zipped over and all around them without inflicting much damage.

"I went down in a mud puddle that time," growled Bart, as he rose dripping.

"I notice you stayed there, though," grinned Tom.

"Any port in a storm," laughed Billy. "There's no time to pick and choose when those ticklers are coming down. It's a case of 'the quick or the dead'."

"I was quick all right," grumbled Tom, as he rubbed his knee, "and I'd almost rather be dead than do it again. See that stone? It got me!"

For some minutes more occasional bombs dropped down over a wide area, especial attention being devoted to the field hospital in accordance with the usual brutal German tactics.

But there were no more casualties, and after awhile the bombardment ceased.

"Guess they're all out of ammunition," conjectured Frank, when at last quiet reigned.

"Either that or our aviators have driven them off as they did this afternoon," returned Bart.

"Let's go back to the mill," Tom suggested. "There'll be plenty of ventilation in the old crib to-night."

"And my cot's right beneath that hole in the roof," grumbled Bart.

"Safest place in the whole shebang," comforted Frank. "Lightning never strikes twice in the same spot."

"Yes, but suppose it rains," grouched Bart.

"Aw, it's good for the complexion," grinned Tom. "Anyway, you're soaked through now, aren't you? Some fellows are never satisfied."

"Ah, stop fighting!" said Frank. "It couldn't rain if it wanted to with a moon like that."

Once back in the mill, the army boys set about repairing the havoc wrought by the bomb.

Billy picked up the banjo, patted it lovingly and was relieved to find that his favorite instrument had come through the German attack uninjured.

"Glad you're all right, old girl," he said, running his fingers over the strings. "But I guess you're through for one night."

"Yes," chuckled Tom, as he started to unlace his shoes. "The Huns have given us their idea of a moonlight serenade!"

CHAPTER XIX

IT might have been expected that a sleepless night would have followed the raid. But the young Americans were far too healthy and their nerves were already becoming too well steeled to let the Germans, like Macbeth, "murder sleep." Their eyes closed almost as soon as their heads touched the pillows, not to open again until reveille sounded the next morning.

They were a little more subdued than usual, however, as they dressed, for there was poor Fred's empty cot and some dark red blotches on the floor to remind them of their comrade's plight and their own narrow escape.

"I wonder how Fred's getting along," said Tom, voicing the general thought.

"All right, I hope," returned Frank. "It will make him sore to be cooped up now with a broken leg, just when the boys are putting the finishing touches on their training."

They were relieved to find on inquiry after breakfast, that Fred was doing finely, that the wound in his head was negligible and that the

153

break in his leg was a simple fracture so that in six weeks he would probably be as well as ever.

"The old scout will have one satisfaction, anyway," said Bart. "He's the first one in our bunch who has actually shed his blood for Uncle Sam."

"Gee, he beat us to it," agreed Tom. "But don't worry, we'll have plenty of chances later on."

In the interval before drill, they strolled about the old mill, seeking traces of the visitation of the night before. These were easily visible for there were immense shell holes where the bombs had buried themselves in the earth.

They found one of the missiles that had not exploded. Bart was about to pick it up when Frank shouted a warning.

"Nix on that funny business!" he cried. "You never can tell when those fellows will start working."

"Yes," added Bart. "Those fingers of yours will come in handy later on. You'll need them in your business."

"Yes," remarked their corporal, Wilson, who sauntered up to them at the moment. "For all we know that thing may have been fixed so that it wouldn't explode when it struck the ground but would the minute somebody picked it up and commenced fooling with it. The only safe way is to give them all a wide berth.

The corporal was popular with the men directly under him, and although he was a strict disciplinarian and kept the men up to their work, there was nothing petty or tyrannical about him. And the respect the men had for him was heightened by the stories that were told in the regiment of the adventures he had undergone.

For he had been a rover over the earth, and in his short life of thirty years had passed through more exciting scenes than fall to the lot of most men in a lifetime. He had been a miner in Australia, had ridden the ranges in Arizona, "mushed" in the Klondike. and been at one time a member of the famous Canadian Mounted Police. He was quiet and reserved, never boasting of his exploits and extremely efficient in anything he set about to do. He was a dead shot and could shoot from the hip with either hand. A coin tossed into the air at a distance of fifty feet he could clip four times out of five.

On one occasion the boys had been astonished eye witnesses of his shooting. The nine of clubs had been pinned to a tree sixty paces distant and Wilson, pulling the trigger so quickly that the eye could scarcely follow, had wiped out the spots in nine successive shots.

He was as courageous as he was skilful, and in case of trouble could be counted on as one of the most valuable members of the regiment.

So that when he showed a disposition to depart from his usual reserve and take part in the conversation the boys made room for him with alacrity.

"Fritz is full of cunning little tricks," the corporal continued. "They played the fountain pen game and got a lot of our fellows before the Allies got wise to it."

"That's a new one on me," said Frank. "What is the fountain pen game?"

"Why," answered Corporal Wilson, as he seated himself comfortably on a nearby rock and struck a match for his pipe, "the Heinies in the first line trenches when our boys went over the top and drove them out used to leave behind them a lot of their stuff because they usually skipped in a hurry.

"One of our boys would find a fountain pen among other things and think he had a prize, but the first time he started to unscrew the cap the thing would explode and smash his hand to bits. We've got a good many cripples in the ranks on account of that. But the game's played out now, and they'll have to think up a new one."

"We ought to get even with them for that," said Tom.

"Oh, we've got even all right," grinned the corporal. "We worked them on the hand grenades. You know how it is sometimes, when the first line trenches are facing each other. A Frenchman or a Britisher throws over a hand grenade, the Hun catches it on the wing, as it were, if its a long time fuse and throws it back in the hope that it will explode in the Allied trenches and thus become a boomerang."

"Rather a risky game I call it," said Billy. "It wouldn't be any fun to have one of those gentle little things go off in your hand."

"That's where the trick comes in," said the Corporal. "You know of course, there are two kinds of fuses. The short time fuse has red threads in it, the long time fuse hasn't. If the German sees that there are none of these red threads in the fuse of the grenade that drops near him he figures he's got time to throw it back.

"Well, one of the British Tommies had a bright idea and he carefully picked all the red threads out of a short time fuse. Then he zipped it over. Of course the Heinie picked it up, thinking it was a long timer and that was about all for Heinie. It blew him and all the men near him to German headquarters."

"To German headquarters," said Bart, wonderingly. "I don't get you."

The corporal grinned.

"Haven't you heard that?" he said. "A British Tommy wrote home that he'd had pretty good luck through the war for he'd sent a dozen Germans to Hades. The British censor scratched out the word, 'Hades' and wrote above it, 'It is not permitted to refer to German headquarters'."

The boys laughed.

"And yet they say the British haven't a sense of humor," commented Frank.

"That's why I say," summed up the corporal, "that you've got to be mighty careful in handling all these contraptions. A fool and his fingers are soon parted."

"Does he mean me?" asked Bart with a grin.

"You've said something," agreed Billy, with unflattering frankness.

The corporal strolled on.

"Fine fellow, that Wilson," remarked Frank.

"He's all of that," agreed Billy, who having been with him when the regiment was on the Mexican border knew him better than his companions did. "That fellow could lick his weight in wildcats. There isn't anything he's afraid to tackle. I heard a story about him once that you fellows wouldn't believe if I told you."

"Let's hear it," said Bart.

"Shoot," chimed in Tom. "We'll see about believing it after we've heard what it is."

"It happened down in Nicaragua," went on Billy. "Caribtown, I think it was, or some place near there. There was some little dinky revolution going on and Wilson it seems had gone down there on some filibustering expedition. He drank pretty freely in those days though he doesn't touch a drop now.

"It seems he was in one of the town resorts when he heard talk about a boa constrictor that had recently been captured and confined in a big cage. The snakes down there don't measure more than ten or twelve feet, but they can easily crush a man if they get their coils around him.

"Wilson just then had got into a condition where he was ready to fight a regiment, and he sneered at their fear of the snake. They egged him on until he boasted that he would be willing to meet the snake in a close room with nothing but a knife. The riffraff there called his bluff and it was arranged that the fight should take place the next morning."

"Some contract!" ejaculated Tom.

"Is this straight goods, Billy, or are you getting us on a string?" asked Bart suspiciously.

"On the dead level," answered Billy. "I had it from a fellow who was down there at the time and knew all about it."

"Stop chinning, you fellows, and let Billy get on with his story," commanded Frank. "He's just getting to the creepy part now and I want to know how the thing turned out."

"Well," continued Billy, "when Wilson woke up the next morning he realized what he was up against. But he was as game as a pebble, and though he knew the odds were against him he wouldn't back out.

"The snake, that had been teased and irritated until it was bursting with rage, was dumped from its cage into a back room of the resort. Then Wilson, armed only with a long knife that they had lent him, went in and shut the door behind him, while the natives crowded around the windows to see the fight.

"The instant the snake saw Wilson he reared up almost to the ceiling and flung himself at the man's throat. Wilson dodged and the fangs caught him in the shoulder. Wilson slashed savagely at the coils that were trying to coil themselves around his body and they staggered around the room. But the knife failed to reach a vital spot and finally one of the folds got around Wilson's legs and he fell to the floor, still stabbing savagely. The snake had won the first round, and it promised to be the last."

There was a gasp from Billy's listeners but their interest was too tense to permit of any interruption.

"Just then," continued Billy, "something happened. One of the natives who had a little more humanity than the rest of the crowd had sculled off to an American gunboat that was lying in the harbor, and told of the scrap that was going to be pulled off. The captain sent over a squad of marines with a rush and they got there just in time to break in the door and hack the snake to pieces with their cutlasses. Another minute and it would have been all over. As it was, Wilson was unconscious, and it was some weeks before he came around shipshape."

"What a daring thing that was to do!" ejaculated Frank.

"He certainly was there with the nerve!" exclaimed Bart.

"I'll bet he hasn't had any use for snakes since then," added Tom.

"In one way it was a good thing," said Billy, "for it made Wilson swear off from drinking and he's never touched liquor since. You see how he is now, as steady as a church."

"Well," commented Bart, "he'll have all the fighting he wants from now on."

"Yes," agreed Frank with a laugh, "with snakes that wear helmets."

"Look who's here, boys!" exclaimed Tom suddenly, as they saw four soldiers approaching with a prisoner under guard.

"Why, it's Nick Rabig!" they exclaimed in unison as they recognized the burly figure that slouched sullenly along between the quartette guarding him.

"What has he been up to, now, I wonder?" questioned Billy curiously as they sauntered forward to intercept the party.

Rabig favored them with a scowl that had rarely been absent from his face since he had been caught in the draft.

"What's the trouble?" asked Frank of the leader of the file, whom he happened to know.

"Insubordination," was the terse response. "Refused to salute an officer."

"Putting him in the jug on general principles," volunteered another, who was more communicative. "He's been shirking ever since he got here."

"A bad egg," added the third. "It's lucky there aren't many of his type among the boys. The Huns would have an easy job if they were all like him."

They passed on to the building that served as a guardhouse, and which, be it said to the credit of the boys in France, had very few inmates. For the discipline of the camp was strict and the spirit of the men was good. They felt that they stood to the French for what America was and they tried to live up to the high standards laid down for them by generations of American ancestors.

"I think that's the best place for Nick," commented Tom as the doors closed behind the prisoner. "He's a surly brute and he might affect others. One rotten apple in a barrel can spoil the whole barrelful."

"He's no good," said Bart. "Remember how he used to talk on the other side? I'll bet at this minute he'd rather be wearing a Prussian helmet than an American uniform."

"Sure thing," said Billy. *'Die Wacht am Rhine'* is the only music he cares to hear."

At this moment Corporal Wilson returned with a paper in his hand upon which he had been noting down the assignments of the day.

"Two of you fellows are in for guard duty," he said, consulting his list. "You, Sheldon, and Raymond will serve till after mess."

He passed on and Bart made a wry face when his back was turned.

"Sweet job!" he muttered.

"Orders are orders," replied Frank, as they shouldered their guns and marched down to the guardhouse.

They began to pace back and forth, exchanging a word now and then at the point where their beats adjoined.

Nick Rabig was lounging at the barred window in an evil temper. If anything could have added to his anger it was the fact that the two young soldiers he most detested had been chosen to stand guard over him and witness his humiliation.

Frank's generous nature sensed the prisoner's feeling, and he studiously avoided catching his glance or taking any notice of him.

But Rabig, incapable of appreciating Frank's motive, chose to interpret this as studied contempt, and his rage flamed forth in a coarse epithet that Frank only half caught but that brought him up all standing.

"What's that you said?" he demanded quickly.

"None of your business!" snarled Rabig, but before the glint in Frank's eyes he did not venture to repeat the insult.

"Now look here, Rabig," said Frank, sternly. "Cut out that sort of stuff. I heard what you said and if you were outside here and weren't in uniform I'd thrash you within an inch of your life."

"Talk is cheap," sneered Rabig. "Why didn't you do it when you were on the other side? You had chance enough."

"I had my reasons," replied Frank, "but they're reasons that a fellow like you couldn't appreciate. As it was, you came within an inch of getting what was coming to you. Some day you will get it, Rabig, and when I cut loose you'll know there's something doing!"

CHAPTER XX

A RATTLING BOUT

Just then the officer of the day approached. Rabig slunk away from the window while Frank resumed his pacing, and the episode ended then and there.

At the end of three days Rabig's term expired and he was sent back again to his place in the ranks, somewhat subdued in manner though really unchastened in spirit.

His hatred of Frank was unabated and in fact seemed to have taken on extra bitterness since the sharp exchange at the guardhouse. He seldom passed Frank without a sneer on his lip or an ugly gleam in his eye, which betrayed the smoldering fires within.

Frank, on his part, bore no rancor. His nature was too open and healthy to nurse a grudge, and although he avoided speaking to Rabig, he seldom thought of him except when the exigencies of military duty threw them together.

"You're as popular as the smallpox with that gink," said Billy one day, after Rabig had passed them with his usual malignant stare at Frank.

"You want to keep your eyes open, Frank," added Tom, who, knowing Rabig better than Billy, distrusted him profoundly. "He's got something up his sleeve."

"I don't think it would be safe to be alongside him in the trenches," put in Bart. "Especially on a dark night. It's an easy thing there to slip a bullet into a man you don't like, and charge it up against the Germans."

"Oh, shucks!" laughed Frank, "Rabig's pretty bad but he isn't as bad as that."

Several weeks went by, weeks of strain and hard work that were rapidly converting the new army into a first-class fighting machine.

But "all work and no play makes Jack a dull boy," and the officers saw to it that there was plenty of entertainment for the men when the hard day's work was over.

There were improvised vaudeville entertainments and, as there were many actors in the ranks, including some whose names were famous, the performances were really good.

Then too, there were boxing matches, which were perhaps the most popular of all. The boys themselves took part in these and there was a good deal of rivalry, all of it good-natured, among the representatives of the various companies and regiments in camp.

The Government had been quick to recognize the value of boxing, not only as a physical exercise, but because it aided vastly in the bayonet drill.

The two contests closely resembled each other and excellence in one meant excellence in both. There was the same sparring for advantage, feinting, alternate advance and retreat, evading and covering up, attacking and defending.

And because of this, every camp had its official boxing instructor and the sport formed part of the regular drill.

Great care was taken to avoid any brutal element. The rounds were limited to two minutes each and the men were cautioned against letting go with all their weight.

It was a matter of points secured by skill, and it was closely akin to a fencing bout with buttons on the foils to avoid any serious injury.

Frank had always had a fondness for the sport even before he joined the army. He and Bart had often put on the gloves in a friendly bout at the Camport gymnasium. He was as quick as a cat on his feet, a good judge of distance, and unerring in picking out the weak points of his opponent's offense.

Under the skillful training that he received

from McGrath, who was a well-known ama-
teur boxer and had been put in charge of the
athletic sports of the camp where the boys
were stationed, he had made surprising progress and was admitted to be easily the best
soldier with the gloves in his own special bat-
talion.

One night a boxing programme had been
staged for Frank's regiment and a series of interesting bouts was looked for.

"Are you going on to-night, Frank?" asked
Bart.

"Yes," Frank replied. "And I feel in dandy
shape. I never felt more full of pep than I
do just now."

"Who's McGrath going to put against you?"
asked Tom.

"I'm slated to meet Thompson, of company
F," replied Frank.

"And he's a crackajack, too," put in Billy.
"He cleaned up the champs of all the other
companies when the old Thirty-seventh was
down on the Mexican border. You've got your
work cut out for you, Frank."

And Billy's prediction was verified, for on
that night Frank found that Thompson was
an opponent to be reckoned with. It was a
slashing, four-round bout with the scales hang-
ing even most of the time, but in the closing

round Frank had a shade the better of it and was announced the victor.

Amid tumultuous handclapping of company B, whose champion he was, Frank waved his hand smilingly and was about to go off the platform when Corporal Wilson, who was acting as master of ceremonies, stopped him with a gesture.

"Pretty well winded, Sheldon?" he asked.

"Not a bit," laughed Frank. "I'm as fresh as a daisy. Like John Paul Jones, I've just begun to fight."

"That's good," smiled Wilson, "because I'm short a match. One of the pair who were to come on after you and Thompson is rather under the weather and the doctor won't let him take part, though he's game as a fighting cock and wants to go on anyway. If you felt in shape for it I thought perhaps you might help out by taking on some other fellow for a few minutes so that the boys won't be disappointed."

"Sure thing," said Frank. "Bring him along."

"I haven't got anyone picked out, just this minute," said the corporal a little perplexedly.

"Send out a call for volunteers," Frank suggested. "It will make it all the more interesting."

"That's the idea," said the corporal. "Any of you fellows want to put on the gloves with Sheldon?" he called out.

There was a momentary hush and then a figure rose from the throng and Nick Rabig pushed his way through to the platform.

CHAPTER XXI

PAYING A DEBT

FRANK gave a start of surprise as he saw who his opponent was to be, and Bart, who was acting as Frank's second, leaned over him with a word of warning.

"Keep your eye peeled, Frank," he advised. "You know what Rabig is and the way he feels toward you. This is just a scheme of his to get even. He isn't coming up here for a friendly bout. He wants to show you up and knock you out if he can."

"Oh, I don't know," said Frank, unconcernedly. "But if he tries on anything like that I'll give him all he's looking for."

Rabig's second, Werner, one of the few friends he had in the regiment and who like himself was suspected of pro-German leanings, or at least lukewarmness in the service, took a long time in putting on his principal's gloves, and Bart, who was watching him with the eye of a hawk, stepped across the platform to witness the operation.

"Let me look at those gloves," he demanded.

"What's the matter with them?" growled Werner.

"This is the matter with them," said Bart, as he pointed to the part just above where the knuckles came and where the stuffing of the glove had been kneaded aside so that a blow given would be almost like one with the bare fist.

"None of that skin-tight business here," said Bart.

He pounded the glove until it was normal and then handed it back, not going to his own corner, however, until they had been fastened on Rabig's hands to his own satisfaction.

"That cur can't play fair in anything," he remarked to Frank as he came back.

The bell rang and the men came from their corners toward the center of the platform.

Frank extended his hand in the customary greeting but Rabig refused to take it. There was a stir in the audience.

"Looks like a grudge fight," remarked one, with quickened interest.

"It does on Rabig's part," assented his neighbor. "But if it comes to that I'm betting on Sheldon to trim him."

The boxers sparred for a moment, Frank cool and smiling, Rabig surly and furious. Then Frank found an opening and landed a deft uppercut that shook Rabig from head to foot.

He rushed at Frank like a mad bull but Frank cleverly side-stepped and countered with a left to the ear. Of the two Rabig was the heavier and in Camport had won a reputation as a rough and tumble fighter.

Stung by Frank's cleverly planted blows, he threw what little science he had to the winds and the next minute the two were at it, hammer and tongs.

"I'll do you!" Rabig panted, as he slugged right and left, vainly endeavoring to get through Frank's guard.

"Go as far as you like," retorted the latter, emphasizing the retort with a left jab that nearly lifted Rabig off his feet.

The bell that announced the end of the round found Rabig winded by his furious endeavors. But Frank, though breathing a little heavily, was serene and confident, as he returned to his corner.

"I told you he was in dead earnest," said Bart, as his principal sat down on his stool for a minute's rest. "Look out for fouls, Frank. He'll do anything to down you."

In the round that followed, Bart's warning was amply justified. Rabig in one of the clinches, as he leaned on Frank's shoulder, tried to bite and he butted continually.

"Cut that out, Rabig," warned Frank in a low tone, after the latter had twice used his head as a battering ram. "My patience won't last forever."

"I'll get you yet!" gasped Rabig.

Once more he drove his head at Frank's chin and the latter, now thoroughly aroused by the foul tactics, let fly his right and caught his burly adversary fairly on the point of the jaw.

Down went Rabig like a shot. Frank generously reached out his hand to help him to his feet, but Rabig struck it away and just here Corporal Wilson intervened.

"That'll do," he commanded. "We don't want any knockout. Sheldon wins."

Frank with a smile and wave of the hand stripped off his gloves and left the platform, to be pounded and mauled in exultation by his admiring comrades.

Meanwhile, Rabig slunk away followed by hisses and jeers at the foul tactics that after all had only resulted in the beating he so richly deserved.

"You trimmed him good, Frank," cried Tom exultantly.

"You went around him like a cooper around a barrel," jubilated Billy.

"I guess if you owed him anything, you've

paid the score," chuckled Bart. "I've been aching for months to see that bully get what was coming to him."

"I didn't want to hurt him," said Frank, good-naturedly. "But when he came butting at me that way and even trying to bite, I simply had to lace him. But even now I haven't a bit of grudge against the fellow."

"He'll sing small after this," prophesied Tom. "But all the same, Frank, keep your weather eye open. He'll do you a mischief if he ever gets the chance."

It was just after the noonday mess the next day, and the boys were chatting in front of the mill, when Frank, looking carelessly down the road, gave a startled exclamation.

"Look what's coming, fellows!" he cried.

They came up all standing and looked in the direction indicated.

"By the great horn spoon!" ejaculated Tom. "Have I got the delirium tremens?"

"It's a nightmare," declared Billy.

Up the dusty road was coming the weirdest creation that the boys had ever seen. It looked like a great hulking rhinoceros. It moved along slowly and ponderously, as though it were straining under a burden too heavy to be borne.

The sun reflected from its sides showed that it was coated with metal. There were openings in the armor through which the muzzles of machine guns protruded. Around its huge wheels there passed what seemed to be a broad endless chain that formed a path on which the wheels traveled. There was no driver to be seen and it came lumbering along like a blind monster feeling its way. But although its progress was leisurely it was sure, and the boys as they watched it gathered an impression of almost irresistible force.

"I've read of the car of Juggernaut," muttered Tom as it came nearer, "and I guess this must be it."

"It's going into the ditch!" exclaimed Bart, as the monster gave a lurch into a deep depression at the side of the road.

"It'll topple over sure!" prophesied Billy.

But the prophecy proved false for the car righted itself from an almost impossible angle and came on as doggedly as before.

Just before it got to where the boys were standing it came to a halt, a door opened and a young fellow of about their own age leaped out.

He was strong and well built, with hair that crisped in curly waves close to his head and a pair of merry blue eyes that spoke of fun and good fellowship.

"Hello, fellows!" he exclaimed, waving the formality of an introduction and wiping the perspiration from his forehead. "My, but it's hot in there!"

They crowded round him in eager curiosity.

"Where did you dig up this rig?" asked Billy. "Is it real or is it all a hideous dream?"

The newcomer laughed.

"You don't seem to be stuck on my pet," he grinned. "I'll admit she isn't much on beauty, but when she comes to scrapping she's a holy terror."

"She looks it," agreed Frank. "I'd hate to have her bump up against me when she was in a bad temper."

"That's the way the Huns feel," laughed their new acquaintance. "They haven't any use for tanks. You ought to see the way we got 'em in the battle of the Somme."

"Were you there?" asked Tom.

"Very much there," was the answer. "This old rascal of mine was right in the thick of it."

"You English have all the luck!" exclaimed Bart enviously.

"English nothing," replied the operator. "I'm an American just as you are. My name is Stone, Will Stone, and I was born in Detroit."

"Bully!" exclaimed Frank, and there was a general handshake and introductions all around.

"But how did you get over here before the rest of us?" queried Bart.

"Well," laughed Will, "you know Windsor in Canada is just across the river from Detroit and I slipped across and enlisted with the Canadian troops. I knew a good deal about automobiles —everybody in Detroit does, because there are so many plants there—and when these tanks were ready for use and they called for volunteers I was Johnny-on-the-spot."

"You chose a hot branch of the service, all right," commented Tom. "If you were looking for excitement I guess you got it."

"You're a good guesser," grinned Will. "When you're climbing over trenches and crashing through walls and rooting up trees, with bullets pattering against the sides like hailstones on a roof, the fellow who can't get enough excitement out of it is pretty hard to please. But come along, you fellows, and I'll show you over the old shebang if you care to look at it."

They needed no second invitation, and for the next half hour there was a volley of questions and answers as they examined the offensive and defensive qualities of the grim monster that had carried consternation into the German ranks.

"Well, so long, fellows," said Will, when at last he climbed into the tank and set its unwieldy bulk in motion. "Here's hoping that we meet again soon."

"In Berlin, if not sooner!" Frank shouted after him.

A few days later one of the French colonels visited the camp. After his formal reception by the American officers he made a tour of inspection, going among the men, looking over the barracks and asking innumerable questions.

There was an absence of pomp and ceremony about him that was characteristic of the French officers who, perhaps more than those of any other nation, live on terms of simple comradeship with their men, and the boys, to use Billy's phrase, "cottoned to him" at once.

Unfortunately he knew little English and as the boys knew still less French, conversation was halting and difficult. The officer's delight then, can be imagined when, on addressing a question to Frank, the latter responded in French as pure as his own.

"Why, my boy," said Colonel Pavet, "you speak as though you were a son of France."

"A stepson, perhaps," replied Frank, smilingly. "For my mother is a daughter of France!"

CHAPTER XXII

A PROMISE OF HELP

THERE was a gratified exclamation from Colonel Pavet, and a new light came into his eyes. The magic name of France had abolished for the moment all distinctions of rank. The officer reached out his hand and took Frank's in a hearty grasp.

"Then you are fighting for two countries," he ejaculated.

"Yes," laughed Frank. "I'm luckier than most of the fellows."

"In what part of the country was your mother born?" asked the colonel with interest.

"In Auvergne," Frank replied.

"In Auvergne," repeated the officer, with vivacity. "Why I come from that part of the country myself. What was your mother's family name?"

"De Latour," said Frank.

"There is another coincidence," cried the colonel. "I know the family well. Their estate was only a few miles south of ours. Her father was an old comrade in arms and served in the same regiment with me when we were stationed in Algiers.

"Many's the time we've ridden and messed and fought together against the Bedouins. He's dead now," he continued, a slight shade crossing his face. "How proud he would have been were he alive to know that his grandson was fighting for France.

"Let me see," he went on. "I've been a long time away from Auvergne but it seems to me that when I was last there, I heard some talk of trouble in settling his estate—some lawsuit or other, that tied the property up. Do you know anything about it?"

"Yes," replied Frank. "My mother has been worrying over it for some time past. She was just about to sail for France to see about it when the war broke out."

He rapidly sketched the details of the legal trouble with which his mother had made him familiar. The officer listened attentively and with marked sympathy.

"It is too bad," said Colonel Pavet. "I will see what I can do. I have a good many friends in Auvergne and there are many, too, who honor the name and memory of De Latour and would do all in their power to help his daughter.

"And when I tell them that their daughter's

son is fighting on our soil they will redouble their efforts. Count on me, my boy. This terrible war may delay matters but I will not forget."

The too parted then, leaving Frank with his heart beating faster at the thought of what might come from this most unexpected meeting.

Now he would have something to write home to his mother that would thrill her heart. That very night the letter should be written, the letter that was so eagerly awaited, always, in that lonely house at Camport, but that this time would receive even a more joyous welcome than usual.

What a strange twist of fate it would prove if this trip to France, undertaken in a spirit of pure patriotism, should reap a double reward in lifting the burden that had weighed upon his mother's heart for years!

One day a sham battle had been planned that embraced a front several miles in length and Frank's company was detailed to take up a position in a wood at the extreme left of the line.

The boys welcomed the assignment, for it was to carry them into a section of the country that had up to now been unfamiliar to them, and it afforded a diversion from the ordinary drill of the training camp.

They set off in high spirits after a hearty breakfast, and after a hike of four miles reached the bit of woodland where they were supposed to await the attack of the enemy.

"Gee!" exclaimed Frank, as he filled his lungs with the balsam of the woods, "this is great. It's enough just to be alive on a glorious morning like this."

"It's a little bit of Eden," declared Bart, as he looked about him. "Listen to those birds singing. If it weren't for the boom of cannon off there you wouldn't know there was such a thing as war in the world."

"Yes," chimed in Tom, "but there was a snake in Eden, and there's another one in the world now, that's got to be scotched before the world can rest in peace."

"Well, these woods have escaped so far," said Billy, as he looked around at the noble elms and birches.

"Yes," assented Bart, "and I guess they're safe. The German tide has come a good way into France, but I have a hunch that it's about spent its force."

"If the Huns get here they'll have to come over our dead bodies," said Tom.

It was some time before, in the plan for the sham battle, the enemy was expected to approach this copse of woods, and, with sentries posted, to detect and give warning of an approach, the rest of the men had been permitted to break ranks and do as they pleased. Some had thrown themselves on the ground in all sorts of sprawling attitudes, others were smoking and chatting together, while still others wandered to the edge of the woods and gazed over the broad plateau that stretched for more than a mile to the left of the woods. The sky was cloudless and the sun was shining brightly.

The monotonous boom of the distant guns, sounding like the roar of waves upon a beach, kept up unceasingly, but the boys had got so used to it that they scarcely noticed it.

But suddenly, among these bass notes came another sound, or series of sounds, sharp, shrill, metallic, which they had already learned to identify as the popping of anti-aircraft guns.

"That sounds as though they had sighted one of the Hun aeroplanes," commented Frank.

"More likely it's part of the practice," remarked Tom, carelessly.

"Look at those shrapnel puffs over there," cried Bart, pointing toward the sky.

High up in the air, following one another in quick succession, were light, bluish streaks, that after reaching an enormous height, suddenly burst in a cloud of white.

"They're certainly firing at something," remarked Billy, "but for the life of me I don't see what it is."

"I do," cried Bart. "Look! just at the edge of that fleecy cloud. It's so white you can hardly tell it from the cloud itself."

They strained their eyes in the direction where Bart was pointing. High up in the air, miles, it seemed, was a long, silver streak, shaped like an immense cigar. At that height it seemed almost to hang in the atmosphere, so gliding and imperceptible was its motion. And yet the boys knew that it was really shooting along with the speed of an express train.

"A Zeppelin!" they shouted, in chorus.

"A super-Zeppelin, or I miss my guess," observed Frank. "Look at the size of it."

"Oh, if the guns could only reach it!" exclaimed Bob.

"No such luck," groaned Billy, "it's too far up. See! the shrapnel puffs are half a mile below it."

"It's on its way back to the German lines," remarked Frank, "and I guess there's nothing to stop its getting there."

"Been on a baby killing trip to Paris, I suppose," said Tom, bitterly.

"More likely London, judging from the direction," estimated Billy.

They watched the monster as it sailed swiftly on, until it was lost to sight.

"I'd have given a year of my life to have seen that thing brought down," said Bart. "Can't you see the crew of it gloating over the women and children they've killed, and boasting about it when they get back to their lines?"

"Well, you know the Indians used to scalp women and children just as eagerly as they did men," remarked Billy, "and those Boches can give the Indians cards and spades and beat them out."

They were about to go back to the grove, with one last regretful look at the sky, when an exclamation from Frank brought them to a sudden halt.

"There's another one," he cried, pointing to the distant horizon. Even as he spoke a second Zeppelin came plainly into view, following in the wake of the first, but with greatly diminished speed.

"Great Scott!" exclaimed Bart, "there must be a fleet of them!"

"That one hasn't got off scot free, either," said Frank, his keen eye noting the apparent distress of the giant airship, as it moved uncertainly and unevenly, like a ship laboring in a storm. "By Jove, fellows, I believe it's coming down! Quick! get under the cover of these trees!"

Lower and lower, like a bird with a broken

wing, the Zeppelin came toward the earth,
while the boys watched it in breathless excitement.

Whether the Zeppelin could go no further,
and sank despite itself, or whether its commander, looking at that broad plateau, and seeing no sign of life upon it, had decided to make
a landing, quickly repair his injured machinery,
and then rise again to seek refuge behind his
own lines, the boys could not tell. But whatever the reason, not many minutes had passed
before it became apparent that the airship was
coming down, inevitably, right in front of them.

The word had been passed quickly all through
the woods, and the whole company was on the
alert.

"Ready for action, men," commanded the
lieutenant.

With rifles in hand, and all their senses
keenly on the alert, the soldiers waited for the
coming of their prey.

With a perceptible jar the airship struck the
ground, and at the same instant her crew
swarmed out and dropped over the sides.

"Charge!" shouted the American lieutenant,
and out from the woods the army boys went
with a rush.

The astounded Germans were taken so utterly by surprise that they stood for a moment

as though paralyzed. Then their commander barked out a sharp order, and two of the men leaped on board and made for the engines.

Crack! went the lieutenant's revolver, and as the bullet whistled past the ears of the foremost man both Germans came to a stop.

"Forward, men, and surround them, but don't shoot unless you have to," was the next order, and an instant later the German crew were ringed about with rifles whose ominous muzzles threatened to mow them down at the first false move.

The German officer had started to draw a pistol, but seeing the uselessness of this, he shoved it back into its holster and shrugged his shoulders. He was trapped. The game was up. He raised his hands in signal of surrender.

Another command from the lieutenant, and the crew were disarmed. A certain number of the men were detailed to guard them, and others were placed in charge of the airship.

The boys were wild with delight at the rich prize that had fallen so unexpectedly into their hands.

"We've had two great days, boys!" exclaimed Frank, "if we never have any others. The day we saw the submarine potted, and the day we nabbed the Zeppelin."

"Glory, hallelujah!" crowed Bart. "And to

think we've got it in such good shape. The Allies have been crazy for a long time to find out just what new wrinkles the Germans have got in the way of machinery and other features in their latest Zeppelins. Maybe the engineers won't come running when they learn of this!"

"And maybe there won't be joy in Paris and London and Washington!" jubilated Tom.

"And perhaps the Huns won't gnash their teeth and tear their hair!" chuckled Billy. "Oh, boy, we sure had luck when they sent us out here this morning."

"That German officer is a hard loser," remarked Frank. "See that scowl on his face. A thundercloud has nothing on him. He's sore through and through."

The boys would have liked nothing better than to have had a chance to explore the Zeppelin and see the many interesting and novel features embodied in it, but their hopes in this direction were doomed to be disappointed. The lieutenant was inflexible in his resolve to have absolutely nothing on the captured airship disturbed until the government experts arrived to inspect it, and sorely against their wills the boys were forced to content themselves with an exterior view of the wonderful fabric.

The German officer, being utterly without

means of escape, had not been put under the custody to which his crew had been subjected. He stood stiffly by the side of the American lieutenant, awaiting the disposition that the latter might choose to make of him.

The American officer sought to question him, but found his prisoner, although able to speak English, inclined to reply only in monosyllables. The courteous persistence of the American, however, had its effect, and the German became more communicative, but he balked at telling where he had been, or what his raid had accomplished. After answering a number of questions of lesser importance, the German himself became the questioner.

"To what enemy have I surrendered?" he queried.

"To a regiment of the United States Army," replied the lieutenant.

A bewildered look came into the prisoner's eyes.

"You mean British Army," he suggested, by way of correction.

"I said United States," said the lieutenant, briefly.

The puzzled look deepened.

"Impossible!" he exclaimed. "There is no United States Army in France."

Despite himself, the American officer could hardly suppress a smile.

"Just listen to him!" exclaimed Frank, who was within hearing distance.

"Didn't I tell you the Germans would believe anything their generals told them?" replied Bart.

"My, but this is rich!" chortled Tom.

"I wouldn't have believed it if I hadn't heard it," chuckled Billy, in a tone too subdued for the lieutenant to notice.

"I assure you," said the lieutenant, "that there is an army of the United States in France, despite your unbelief. Why should it seem so strange?"

"But you couldn't possibly have gotten over here," persisted the prisoner.

"Why not?" asked the American.

"Because our U-boats would have stopped you," was the reply.

"No use," murmured Frank to Bart. "Nobody home."

"Padded cell number nine hundred and ninety-nine," whispered Billy.

It was of no use to argue against such credulity, and the lieutenant gave it up.

The prisoners were marched back to camp, where the news of their coming had preceded them. It created a great sensation, and was the main topic of conversation for many days thereafter.

"It's been a red letter day," remarked Bart

that night, as he prepared to climb into his bunk.

"You bet it has," agreed Frank. "We bagged a Zeppelin!"

Two days after these momentous events, a stir of expectation ran through the camp. Evidently some important move was in prospect. What it was, the rank and file did not know, but rumors and conjectures ran riot.

"There's something big coming, boys," said Frank, one night after supper.

"That's plain enough," agreed Bart. "But I'd give a lot to know just what it is."

"The corporal gave me a private tip," replied Frank. "He didn't go very far into it, but from what he hinted I have a hunch that none of us will go to bed to-night."

"What?" they cried, in chorus.

"That's what," returned Frank. "But of course it may be a false alarm. Wilson himself wasn't any too sure."

An hour later the bugle blew, but this call was not for "lights out." It was the command to "fall in."

Sudden as it was, the high state of discipline the men had reached was shown by the fact that there was no confusion. As precisely as veteran soldiers they fell into line by companies and platoons and waited for the order "Forward, march!"

The order was not long in coming, and as quietly as ghosts, with no band to lead them, the regiment swung into step and started off.

"We're on our way to the front," whispered Frank to Bart, who marched on his right.

"Off to the trenches!" agreed Bart. "Well, I'm glad the waiting time is over. Now, we'll have a chance to show what kind of soldiers we are."

For three whole hours the march went on without a halt. The night was clear although there was no moon. As the ground was dry and springy the going was good.

During that last hour the signs had multiplied that they were approaching the scene of battle. They passed by bits of woodland where every leaf and twig had been stripped from the trees by shell fire, leaving only the scarred and ghastly trunks.

They went through villages, or what had once been villages, but were now only heaps of crumbling stone with, here and there, a shaky wall left standing.

They had to watch their footing more and more to avoid falling into craters where the ground had been torn up by shells. There was no beauty in that part of fertile France that had once been like a "garden of the Lord." War had breathed upon it, blighting and blasting every living thing, except the dauntless spirit of the people who were fighting and would fight to the last gasp in defense of liberty and civilization.

At last they reached a line of sentinels by whom they were greeted, not with challenges, but with exclamations of delight and welcome.

A little further on they came to a great gash in the earth that stretched in either direction like a huge black, zigzag blot.

They had reached the trenches!

But they did not stop there. Onward they went again, past another line of trenches.

"Gee! we must be going to the first line of trenches!" whispered Bart.

"That's what!" answered Frank.

CHAPTER XXIII

FACING THE HUN

JUST this side of one of the lines of trenches the regiment halted at the word of the commander. Then it stood at attention and presented arms while from out the trenches came an endless line of men who had held that trench for France and now were yielding their place to the ardent young soldiers of the sister republic across the sea.

There was a strong impulse to cheer on both sides, but that might have betrayed to the enemy the change that was taking place in that sector of the line, and this for strategic reasons, it was desirable to avoid.

Soon the last of the war-worn veterans was lost in the darkness. Then, with infinite caution the boys of the old Thirty-seventh marched into the trenches, guided only by lanterns that waved low before them like so many fireflies.

So perfectly the movement had been planned, so carefully had been mapped out in advance the exact location that each unit of the command was to occupy, that, within an hour after the substitution had been made, the entire regiment was placed, and, apart from those detailed for duty, was sound asleep!

Curiosity ran riot when the army boys woke in their unfamiliar surroundings. At last they had reached the trenches, that magic word that they had heard again and again in the daily discussions of the last three years, and they studied every detail of their new surroundings with the keenest interest and zest.

Here they were to live, here some of them, beyond a question, were to die. The thought was sobering, and on that first day there was little of the gaiety and jest that had marked their life in the camps behind.

"Well, Bart, old scout, we're in for it now," said Frank, after breakfast, as he placed his hand on his friend's shoulder.

"In for fair," responded Bart.

"We're up against the real thing," added Billy. "We had a little taste of trench life down in Mexico, but most of the life was in the open. This is a different proposition."

Just then a shell came screaming overhead and the boys involuntarily ducked.

"That seems to prove it," said Tom.

"Bad shooting though," remarked Frank, coolly. "Fritz ought to have the range better by this time."

"There isn't very much of that sort of thing

going on just now," remarked Corporal Wilson, who came along just then. "This is what they call a 'quiet sector.' The boys are just put here to be broken in and get used to the sight and sound of the shells. This is a deaf and dumb asylum compared to what you'll get later on."

"Job's comforter," murmured Bart. "To hear the corporal talk you'd think this was a rest cure."

In the hours of liberty allowed them the army boys explored the trenches for a long distance in either direction, and what they saw tended to upset a good many of the notions they had formed.

In a vague way they had figured the trench to be not much else than a gigantic ditch. They found it to be an underground city.

There was a bewildering labyrinth of passages branching off in every direction. There were spacious rooms, fitted up in homely comfort, some with pictures on the walls and rugs upon the floors.

There were shower baths and laundries, rude in construction but efficient in operation. The sleeping quarters of the men consisted chiefly of bunks, rising in tiers, though in some cases, cots were used.

There was an apparently endless series of

communicating trenches with the listening posts in advance of the main line. There were telephone wires and electric lights.

"The moles have got nothing on us," remarked Tom, as he noted the vast extent of these subterranean passages.

"It's like the catacombs of Rome," put in Billy. "The only difference is that those contain dead men while we're very much alive."

"Knock wood," counseled Bart. "We wouldn't be very long if the Boches had their way."

Along the side of the main trench, facing the enemy was a narrow platform on which the men stood who were on watch. A series of cunningly contrived loopholes enabled them to look over at the enemy trenches without themselves being seen.

Sand bags were piled on the top of the trench in numbers sufficient to stop the flight of a bullet or even the impact of a shell.

A series of steps led up to the top and the boys reflected as they looked at them that before long their feet would be planted there when the order should be given to go *"over the top"* and charge across the intervening space to meet the enemy.

The silent men standing on watch, gripping their muskets, their eyes peering through the loopholes, seemed like so many statues.

Each had his gas mask ready to clap on at an instant's notice, for when that deadly poison should be wafted over the trench, one second of time might mean all the difference between life and death.

Before the day was over Frank and his comrades had replaced this line of sentinels. They peered curiously across to the German trench from which they were separated by not more than two hundred yards.

There was absolutely nothing to be seen except the line of sand bags that they knew marked the positions of the enemy. Nothing broke the monotonous expanse of shell-torn earth.

They had an uncanny feeling as though they were the only living creatures left in the world.

"It looks as though all the Germans had gone back to Berlin," remarked Frank in an undertone.

"Does it?" said the corporal grimly. "Give me your hat."

He took the hat that Frank extended and lifted it above the parapet on the point of a bayonet.

Zip! came a bullet, missing the helmet by a hair and thudding into one of the sand bags.

"Take it all back," said Frank as he resumed his hat. "They're on the job!"

A week passed by with only two casualties on the American side, for the sector was indeed a quiet one. But certain signs of a projected movement on the part of the enemy had made the American officers uneasy, and one day Corporal Wilson called Frank apart.

"Sheldon," he said, "Captain Baker has ordered me to take a squad of men on the first dark or foggy night for patrol duty in No Man's Land. I want you, Raymond, Bradford and Waldon to go with me."

"Good," said Frank, promptly. "We'll be ready."

He sought out his comrades and eagerly imparted the information. They received it with delight.

"Bully!" cried Bart.

"Best news I''ve heard since Hector was a pup!" chortled Billy.

"Here's hoping we'll slip one over on Fritz!" chuckled Tom, gleefully.

CHAPTER XXIV

IN NO MAN'S LAND.

It was a misty, muddy night upon which the reconnoitering party, including Frank, Bart, Billy and Tom, was sent out under Corporal Wilson, with orders to get as close as possible to the enemy's line and learn all they could regarding their positions.

This included information in regard to the general direction of the enemy trenches, the extent and strength of his barbed wire entanglements and, if possible, the approximate force with which the trenches were manned.

Of course, this order involved taking pretty long chances, but the picked men sent out did not give much thought to that side of the question. By now it was all, not only a part of the day's work to them, but the excitement of such an expedition was, in truth, something of a relief from the growing monotony of trench life.

They left their own trenches with the least possible sound and crept cautiously forward toward the enemy defences. The night was heavy and starless, an excellent one for their project.

The soft earth deadened their footsteps and they slipped forward like a company of ghosts, hardly a sound breaking the stillness save the distant roar of the heavy guns that caused the ground to quiver and tremble under their feet.

The mist enveloping them began to grow denser minute by minute and before they had gone more than a hundred yards it was with the greatest difficulty that they kept from becoming separated.

It was an uncanny experience for the young, almost untried soldiers, and the Camport boys were excited, and each eager to prove himself worthy of having been chosen for the work.

Suddenly Frank thought he heard a subdued sound on his right and instinctively stopped a moment to locate it more definitely.

In that second his comrades, who apparently had heard nothing, were swallowed up in the thickening fog. Frank's impulse was to hasten after them but he had hardly taken a step forward when he was again halted by a repetition of the noise he had heard before.

He dared not call out to his comrades as he knew that such a cry would betray them all in case they were near the enemy trenches. His next thought was to return to his own lines, but the sound he had heard, surprisingly like the low-pitched gutturals of a German voice, made him unwilling to go back without investigating the matter further. Besides, here was the beginning of an adventure after his own heart, and he thought with a quickening pulse of the satisfaction that would be his if he could, unaided, gather valuable information and take it back to his commanding officer.

This reflection decided him and slowly and with infinite caution he stole in the direction from which the sounds seemed to come.

He had not gone far when his first impression was verified. Through the mist he heard distinctly the subdued sound of voices. Creeping on still farther as quietly and stealthily as a jungle animal, he could finally catch the articulation in the voices, and he knew the language spoken was German.

"I must be mighty near their entanglements by this time," he thought excitedly. "If I can only get through them I ought to be able to hear something. Here goes for a try at it anyway."

He dropped to hands and knees, regardless of the sticky mud, and wormed his way along, one hand outstretched feeling for the wire that he knew must be close. Sure enough he had not gone ten feet when his hand came in contact with the wire. He dropped flat on the ground and carefully drew his wire cutters from his belt. Cautiously he nipped a section out of the lowest strand and crawled beneath. He knew that he would soon come to a second line, and when he reached it he cut it in the same way he had the first, and then cut a third and a fourth.

"That's probably the last fence," he thought, nor was he mistaken.

He was now close to the enemy's trench and could hear the subdued murmur of voices. Above these came every now and then a sharp word of command and the click of gun mechanisms being inspected together with other sounds indicating a state of bustle and preparation.

To Frank lying prone on the miry ground, these sounds conveyed a very definite and significant message.

"They're up to something sure as shooting!" he thought. "I'll bet they're preparing for an attack on our trenches! They're all as busy as bees!"

He lay quiet a minute longer until the sounds of preparation increased to such an extent that he felt sure the Germans would soon be on the move.

"About time for me to hunt cover," he

thought with a grin that even his perilous position could not repress. "The sooner I get out of this and warn our men the better it will be."

With this thought in mind he turned cautiously about and had started back when suddenly he saw something that made his heart lose a beat.

All over the wire entanglements that lay across his path of escape long sparks were leaping and hissing with a subdued crackling sound like the snapping of a wood fire. The Germans had electricified their wires in the hope of entrapping any scouting party of Americans who might chance to penetrate them!

Now indeed Frank found himself in a terrible predicament. He knew that in the maze of wires he could hardly hope to find the place where he had entered, and he was sure that with the heavy current in the wires it would be certain death to touch them with his clippers. On the other hand he knew that the current would be shut off only a minute or so before the Boches left their trenches to attack. He would hardly have time to cut his way out before being discovered and shot.

However his only chance seemed to be to lie still and await developments. This he did, resolving to make a dash the second the current was cut off.

As he lay there his ears caught the sound of measured footsteps approaching him.

"It's a sentry!" flashed through his mind. His hand flew to the bayonet at his side and he prepared to strike quick and hard.

But then another thought came to him. There must be a way through the entanglements that the Germans used. If he could capture the sentry he might be able to make him act as a guide.

It was a chance—and a desperate chance. Would the sentry prove to be alert and resourceful? Would his love of the Fatherland, or at least his training that the individual must be always subservient to the government, cause him to give the alarm at the expense of his personal safety? Or would he be slow to think and act, and would the very training, having undermined his self-reliance, make him yield to the quick intelligence and the poise that freedom had given to the American?

Noiselessly he shifted his hand to his revolver and drew it forth. He knew that it would be fatal to risk a shot, but he grasped the barrel of the weapon and as the heavy footsteps came abreast of him leaped to his feet and brought the butt down with stunning force on the head of the dim stolid figure that loomed through the mist.

The man dropped without a cry but Frank listened anxiously to judge if the sound of his fall had reached the trenches. Apparently it had not, and satisfied of this the young American turned his attention to the inert figure at his feet.

Presently the man stirred and then in a dazed fashion started to struggle to his feet. Quick as lightning the cold muzzle of Frank's revolver was pressed against the German's neck speaking a language that all men understand. The soldier stood quite still and Frank felt that the man, unstrung by the unexpected attack, would not risk death by giving an alarm.

He was at a loss to convey a command to the German to show him the way out through the barbed wire. He knew little of the German language. But it occurred to him that possibly the German could speak English.

"Show me the way out of this," he commanded, speaking very slowly. "Do you understand?"

"*Yah, yah,*" mumbled the German. "I vill show you, only don't shoot. Dis way. Follow me."

"I'll follow you and mighty close too," Frank assured him. "One false move and you'll never make another."

The German made no reply but crawled sullenly through the mud, Frank following with the muzzle of the gun pressing the man's leg.

Soon the German paused at what appeared to be a sort of gate but would have seemed like any part of the fence to one not acquainted with it. After a moment's fumbling the gate swung open and captor and captive crawled through. In the same way they got through the other lines of wire. Frank was once more in the open and the proud possessor of a prisoner besides.

"Forward march!" commanded the young American. "We will now visit those pigs of Yankees you fellows are so fond of talking about. I know they will be glad to see you."

The big German only hunched his shoulders and went on doggedly. In a little while they were near the American trenches and after answering the sentry's challenge they clambered down.

Frank was met with a wild rush by Bart, Billy and Tom, who had been almost crazy with anxiety because of his failure to return.

"Where have you been, Frank?" shouted Bart, "and where did you get the Boche?"

"I'll tell you when I get back, fellows," promised Frank. "Take care of this Hun. I've got to report right away. I think the Huns are going to attack."

He hurried away and made his report.

"You've done well, very well," declared Captain Baker. "And if the enemy attacks, as you think likely, they will find us ready for them. You may return to your company."

Frank saluted and hastened back. Orders were issued, and soon every man was at his post, strung up to the highest pitch of excitement and expectancy. They strained their eyes through the baffling fog but for a while could see or hear nothing.

Then suddenly a white shaft of light stabbed through the fog and piercing the damp folds revealed row after row of helmeted figures moving toward them with a deliberation and menacing weight that might well have struck terror to hearts less stout than theirs!

CHAPTER XXV

A GALLANT EXPLOIT

CROUCHED, tense, ready for the word, the American lads faced the foe. A thrill of impatience ran through them as the enemy came nearer.

Were they to wait there, until that grey wave overwhelmed them, pouring into the trenches like a surging flood?

The strain of waiting was becoming almost unbearable.

The captain shouted a command, and up they scrambled like hounds freed from the leash. But just as their leader reached the top he fell headlong, stricken by a bullet.

For a moment the men waited, uncertain, hardly knowing what to do. Frank sensed the hesitation and like lightning he acted.

It was no time to consider rank with that grey mass surging on. Above the noise his voice rang out like a trumpet.

"Come on, boys!" he shouted. "Over the top and at them!"

At the same instant he leaped forward and

his comrades followed. On they rushed like an avalanche let loose. They were at Yankee fighting pitch.

All the pent-up rage that had been gathering for months leaped to the fore. The fire that had stirred their ancestors at Bunker Hill and Gettysburg burst into flame.

Wounds? They scorned them. Death? They laughed at it!

On they went like so many vikings. Faster, faster, rushing, pouring onward—until with tremendous force they fell like a thunderbolt upon the advancing ranks.

Into that grey mass they forced their way, shooting, thrusting, stabbing. And when their guns were empty, or they could not use their bayonets, they grasped the weapons and swung them about their heads like flails.

There was a red mist before their eyes and red patches on their tunics. Some of them fell but the others kept on stabbing, hacking, hewing their way into the solid mass until that mass, veteran, as it was, wavered and broke before the wild, irresistible charge.

Slowly at first, then more swiftly, the enemy retreated, pursued to the very edge of their trenches by the American boys, who, having tasted blood, were not to be denied.

They would have gone further but this was

not in the plan of their commanders, for the enemy's guns had got the range and a murderous fire was being laid down.

The enemy had had a trouncing that he would not soon forget. The recall sounded, and the American boys turned back, reluctantly, gathering up their wounded comrades as they came.

Frank had been separated from his chums in the wild melee, and his first thought as he neared the home trench was for their safety. His relief was great when he found them, blackened, panting, their clothing riddled, but they themselves unharmed, except for a slight wound that Tom had received from a bullet that scarcely more than grazed his arm.

Now that the reaction was upon them, they felt unspeakably weary, for nerve and brawn had been taxed to the utmost. But in their eyes glowed the light of victory. They had met the veteran troops of the Kaiser and given them a taste of Yankee mettle.

It was their first battle and they had borne themselves like men.

Once more in the trenches and Tom's slight wound attended to, they peered curiously over the scene of battle. They shuddered as they looked, for there were still forms lying there that had not been there when the battle began.

Who of their own number had gone? Who from that group of jolly, eager, vigorous young manhood with whom they had been living and training for weeks and months—those whom they had come to like and respect as they toiled and pleasured side by side in the camp and in the trenches?

And yet, not one of those who had come back alive from that awful field, where had been left some of their comrades, but would have gladly given his own life that selfishness, arrogance, and brutality should not conquer and rule in this world.

But they took comfort from the fact that despite their own losses, which had been numerous, the greater proportion of those still forms were German.

The enemy's gun fire was still sending a rain of death across the intervening space and the American guns were answering with equal vigor.

It seemed as though no living thing could endure on that infernal plain.

Suddenly Frank's keen eyes detected a movement on the part of one of the apparently lifeless bodies and he gave a sharp exclamation.

"Look there, Bart!" he said. "There's a man still alive. See how he's trying to get up on his elbow—and he's one of our men, too.

That is, he's French—I can tell by his uniform," he added in great excitement, as the light from a bursting star shell threw a ghastly radiance over the field.

The next instant he was clambering up the side of the trench.

"Frank! Frank!" cried Bart desperately, clutching at him. "What are you doing? Where are you going? It's certain death out there!"

"I'm going, Bart," gritted Frank between his teeth as he tore away from his friend's grasp, and leaped over the top!

An instant more and he was on his hands and knees, making his way toward the stricken man who was about twenty yards distant.

Around him bullets rained. A pain shot through his shoulder as though he had been stabbed by a red hot knife, but he kept on doggedly, reached the wounded man and tried to lift him to his feet.

But the effort was futile for the man sank back with a groan. Like a flash Frank's muscular arms lifted him, threw him over his shoulder and staggering, tripping, stumbling, yet somehow keeping his feet, he reached the edge of the trench.

A dozen eager hands relieved him of his burden and then he himself tumbled in, to be caught by Bart and Billy.

What happened in the next half hour, Frank scarcely knew. The wound in his shoulder though not serious had bled freely, and his tremendous efforts had taxed his strength to the utmost.

His surprise was great when, having had his wound attended to, he was ushered into the presence of the man he had saved.

"Why, it is Colonel Pavot!" he gasped.

Of course the French military man was equally amazed.

"It is fate!" he cried. "Fate, nothing less, my brave boy! How can I ever thank you!"

"You don't have to thank me," returned Frank modestly.

"But I shall," and the French colonel grasped the young soldier's hand tightly. He was still very weak and spoke with difficulty.

"I am glad it was you, Sir," remarked the army boy.

"It is fate, I tell you," murmured the colonel. "When I am well I shall tell you more. I have heard from Auvergne, and all about the De Latour estate, which is in the courts. You may have a fight to get your rights, but—I am your friend. I shall fight for you and your mother."

"Then you think my mother's chances are good?" questioned Frank eagerly.

"I am certain of it," was the colonel's low

reply. Then he had to stop talking, by the doctor's orders.

And what was done in the near future to recover the estate, and how Frank and his chum did their further duty as American soldiers, will be told in the next volume, to be entitled: "Army Boys in the French Trenches; Or, Hand to Hand Fights with the Enemy."

When Frank came back to camp his friends hailed him as a veritable hero.

"You're the goods!" cried Billy.

"All wool and a yard wide!" came from Tom.

"And American to the backbone, don't forget that!" added Bart.

THE END